TIED TO A BOSS 2

A Novel

J. L. Rose

Good 2 Go Publishing

TIED TO A BOSS 2
Written by J L Rose
Cover design: Davida Baldwin
Typesetting: Mychea
ISBN: 9781943686667

Copyright ©2016 Good2Go Publishing
Published 2016 by Good2Go Publishing
7311 W. Glass Lane • Laveen, AZ 85339
www.good2gopublishing.com
https://twitter.com/good2gobooks
G2G@good2gopublishing.com
www.facebook.com/good2gopublishing
www.instagram.com/good2gopublishing

Printed in the USA

TIED TO A BOSS 2

A Novel

J. L. Rose

ACKNOWLEDGEMENTS

First I would like to start this by thanking my heavenly father for this great blessing I've been given. To my family that stood with me and continues to support me no matter my mistakes, I thank you and love you.

To my new family, the entire Good2go Publishing for taking a chance and believing in me. I promise I won't stop until I get us some best sellers. To my uncle William "Peanut" Rose. I'm happy to see you still holding me down play boy. I love you man. To my mom (Mrs. Ludie Rose) and to my father (Mr John L. Rose Senior) I Love the two of you next to god who is number one in my life which makes you number two. But lastly I would like to thank my Fan's and there support and love. I promise to get better and give you all the best of me. Just stay tuned....

Peace and Love

DEDICATION

This book is dedicated to my grandmother's Rosa Mae Rose, Gloria Anderson. I miss and love you both. Rest in peace with the lord.

PROLOGUE

After their decision to bring both teams together and rewrite the drug game that no hustler would ever dream possible, Miami's deadliest jack boy, Dante Blackwell, and Dope Girl, Alinna Rodriguez, will turn all of Miami into their empire.

Sick of Dante's secretive ways, Alinna finds herself uncertain after allowing herself to fall for him and dealing with the pressure of running the drug business part of the family, Alinna not only finds herself unable to trust the man she loves, but she questions his love for her.

Dealing with Homicide Detective and baby's mother, Angela Perez, along with the supposed love she claimed to have for him, Dante may be kicked out of the family once Alinna learns of his infidelity. After a planned job in Phoenix turns into him being offered a job as Arizona's biggest drug kingpin, he has to make a decision to take the drug lord's offer or stay in Miami with his family.

Unknown to both Alinna and Dante, new problems are arising in Miami while old problems continue to plague the family. Will Dante and Alinna reconstruct their family in time to figure out who's responsible for the plot against them, or will everything they built together be destroyed?

1

Driving with more thoughts on his mind than were needed and feeling how tired his body was as he drove, he headed home after leaving his daughter's mother, Angela's house dealing with his sick and non-stop crying little girl, walking, laying, and even giving his daughter a cool water bath to cool down her overheated body until both he and Angela were forced to take their daughter to the hospital and to find out that Mya Blackwell was sick with the flu. Dante shook his head, clearing his mind of thoughts of his daughter only for thoughts of Alinna to pop up into his mind.

Dante knew that Alinna had followed him when he went to help Angela with their child because he had seen her BMW follow him and park outside Angela's place. He was surprised when she didn't angrily show up at her front door and had noticed that her BMW was gone by the time he and Angela left to take their child to the hospital.

Finally making it back to the house after leaving Angela's house, Dante parked the Range Rover out front instead of the garage.

Locking up the SUV, he walked over to the front door, unlocked it, and stepped inside. He noticed that most of the lights were out and it was still as silent as it was when he left.

After locking the door behind him, he headed upstairs. He walked down the hallway and stepped inside their bedroom where he found Alinna laying down facing the opposite wall to the bedroom door. Dante attempted to be quick as possible as he sat down his cell and keys.

"Don't climb your nasty ass up into my bed smelling like that bitch. Get your ass in the shower."

Staring at Alinna's form under the thick blanket for a few minutes, Dante shook his head and ignored her comment as he walked around to his side of the bed.

"Nigga, I'm not playing with you!" Alinna said nastily, turning over to face Dante with an offensive look to match the way that she sounded. "You not about to go fuck that bitch and just come hop back in my bed. You must of lost your fucking mind completely."

Sighing deeply, Dante started, "Alinna, look! It's not how you think . . ."

"I don't wanna hear the bullshit!" Alinna yelled, cutting Dante off. "Nigga, you ain't nothing but a lying-ass, bitch nigga. I followed your ass right to that Spanish bitch's house. So don't be lying, Dante. You know what, nigga? Just get the fuck out! Since that bitch the one you want, go be with her ass. You ain't never gotta come back here because I don't want your ass no more. It's over!"

Opening his mouth to say something, but unable to find the right words after standing and hearing the shit Alinna just told him, and just how easily she ended things, Dante finally spoke up asking, "So that's it, huh?"

"Did it sound like I made a fucking mistake, nigga?" she asked, staring hard at Dante. "Get your shit and get the fuck out of my fucking house, Dante! I won't ask you again, nigga!"

Nodding his head slowly as he held Alinna's eyes, Dante simply said, "Alright!" He turned and walked back over to his keys and cell phone and then headed toward the bedroom door.

Watching Dante as he walked out of their bedroom, Alinna broke down crying, falling face down onto her bed while crying into her pillow.

Rolling over onto her back and staring up at the ceiling as tears slid down her face, Alinna felt a scream building up inside of her. But she fought it down as she thought about the way that Dante allowed his so-called daughter's mother to kiss him. She was pretty sure he also fucked the bitch right after supposedly "making love" to her.

"Fuck that lying ass, nigga!" Alinna said out loud, throwing off the blanket, climbing out of bed, and heading straight to the bathroom.

* * *

Not bothering trying to get any sleep, Alinna showered and got herself together. She dressed in blue fitted jeans and a white and blue Gucci t-shirt.

Heading downstairs to the kitchen, Alinna put together something light to eat and then sat at the breakfast bar only to find herself struggling to eat the food she had cooked up.

"Good morning, Ms. Rodriquez," her maid Rose said as she entered the kitchen carrying D.J., who smiled a big smile when he saw his mother.

"Morning, Rose," Alinna replied, pushing her plate of food away. "Why don't you let me hold D.J.?"

"I was just about to feed him," Rose told her as Harmony walked inside the kitchen.

"Hey Rose!" Harmony spoke to the maid, as she looked back over to her girl in front of the refrigerator. "What you doing up so early, Alinna?"

Shaking her head in response to Harmony's question, Alinna changed the subject by asking, "What's up with Raul? You heard anything else from him yet?"

"After the bullshit? No!" Harmony answered, as she moved over and sat beside Alinna. "I thought Dante was handling that issue?"

Feeling her anger building again just from the mention of Dante's name, Alinna never had the chance of answering as Vanessa walked into the kitchen followed shortly by Dre.

"What's up, y'all?" Dre asked, as he walked straight to the refrigerator.

"Alinna!" Vanessa said, stopping beside Alinna at the breakfast bar. "Dante's gone already? I stopped by y'all room and didn't see you or him."

"Look!" Alinna started, taking a deep breath and then blowing it out. "Dante not here. He's not coming back and don't ask me why."

"Why isn't he coming back?" Vanessa asked, ignoring both Alinna's demand and the way she was now staring at her. "What happened, Alinna?"

"Morning everybody!" Wesley said, as he walked into the kitchen, interrupting Vanessa's questions. He turned to Alinna, "Is me brethren wake? Me have information for dem boy."

"Wesley, wait a minute!" Vanessa told him, looking from Wesley back to Alinna and saying, "Alinna was just about to explain to us what's going on with Dante."

Looking from Vanessa and staring at the others as they stood or sat staring back at her, Alinna explained that she and Dante got into a fight and that they both decided that he would move out of the house.

"So basically what you saying is that you kicked my brother out into the street, right?" Dre asked, staring hard at Alinna.

"Andre!" Vanessa said, looking over to her mom.

"Naw!" Alinna spoke up, staring straight back at Dre. She continued, "If Dre wanna know the truth, then I'll tell it to him. His so-called brother ain't shit. He can't keep his dick outta that bitch he got a daughter with. And before anyone of y'all try to defend his ass, know that I'm not just talking. I followed his ass over to the bitch house last night."

"Wait a minute!" Harmony said, just as Dre walked out of the kitchen. Vanessa followed right behind him. "You said you followed Dante to his daughter's mama house last night?"

"She called his ass right after we had sex and his ass jumped right up and ran his ass over to that bitch house. And he didn't get home until a few hours ago."

"What makes you think . . ."

"Hey, y'all," Amber interrupted, as she walked inside the kitchen. "What's up with Dante and Vanessa?"

"I'll explain later!" Harmony told Amber, but then looked back to Alinna asking, "Alinna, look, I 'm not sure exactly what went on between you and Dante, but by you putting him out, where does that leave us with business? You know that if Dante's gone, then most likely Dre and Tony T is gonna follow him. That's their boy, whether Tony T, my man, and Dre's Vanessa's baby daddy or not. What are we gonna do about that now?"

Admitting to herself that she hadn't thought about any of what Harmony was saying and only Dante's disloyalty to her, Alinna looked to Harmony, saying after a moment, "We'll figure out something, Harmony."

* * *

Vanessa listened to Dante explain that Alinna wanted him out of the house, but he seemed uninterested in the reasons she gave and whether they were actually true or not.

Vanessa changed the subject, tuning the conversation to business, "So that's it, Dante? You just gonna leave us with no way to keep up the business? You know that you, Dre, and Tony T was our main source of connect to what we was getting. What are we supposed to do now?"

After a few moments Dante sighed into the phone and said, "Alright, Vanessa. I'ma still take care business on my end, but you're my direct contact for what goes on inside the business. I wanna know everything."

"What about Andre?"

"I got other plans with Dre. But tell Wesley I want 'em to hit me up."

"Where you staying at?"

"I haven't decided but I'll let you know when I find me a spot."

"What about D.J.?"

"I'ma need you to play middleman and bring my son where I'm at. You agree to that, Vanessa?"

Nodding her head but realizing he couldn't see her, Vanessa answered, "I got you, Dante. Just make sure you call me and let me know where you at."

"I'ma call!" he told her. Then he said, "You don't need to tell ya girl where I'm at either."

Hearing Dante hang up the phone, Vanessa looked at her cell phone screen and shook her head. She turned and left her and Dre's bedroom heading back downstairs.

Looking for Dre once downstairs, and seeing both Tony T and Wesley gone while Dre sat inside the den with their son, A.J. watching an X-Men cartoon, Vanessa stopped in the room's opening and said, "Andre, where everybody at?"

"Wesley and Amber went somewhere and Harmony left a few minutes ago with you girl, Alinna somewhere," Dre told his baby mama while rubbing his son's head and staring at the widescreen TV.

Sighing as she entered the den Vanessa dropping down onto the sofa beside Dre. She leaned into her man's side, saying after a silent moment, "I talked to Dante."

"I know. He texted me and told me."

"What else he told you?'

"I'm meeting up with 'em a little bit later on today. We supposed to be planning a trip out to Arizona."

"Where at in Arizona?"

"Phoenix."

"Haven't y'all already been there?"

"Maybe!" Dre answered while shrugging his shoulders still focused on the cartoon. "Dante normally remembers stuff like that."

"You need to start paying attention to it, too," Vanessa told him, taking her son from his father's lap. Standing from the sofa she continued, "I'm taking A.J. to Rose. I want you to go with me somewhere real quick."

Leaving the hotel that he was checked into and driving back across town and meeting up with Angela at her request to discuss something important, Dante pulled the Range Rover into the coffee shop parking lot. He easily found a spot inside the half-empty lot, shut off the SUV, climbed out, and locked up the Range Rover behind him.

Leaving the parking lot and walking over to the coffee shop's front entrance, Dante entered the shop, hearing his name as soon as he stepped through the door.

Seeing Angela seated at a booth next to the window that overlooked the front parking lot, Dante headed over in her direction.

"Hey baby!" Angela said, smiling as she stood up to kiss and then hug Dante.

"What's up, Angela?" Dante replied, sitting down across from her.

Hearing and seeing how tired Dante looked, Angela reached over and grabbed Dante's hand inside both hers. She asked, "Papi, what's the matter? You don't look so good."

"I'm just a lil tired, Angela," Dante answered. "What's up, though? What you wanna talk to me about?"

Staring worriedly at Dante a moment, Angela continued holding his hand, sighed, and then said, "I had a meeting this morning with the Chief of Police. They're still investigating Captain Whitehead's murder."

"They have any leads?"

"As of right now, no!"

"So what's the problem?"

"The problem is that I've just found out that the DEA is in on the case now, too. And the added problem is that the lead agent is Captain Whitehead's son. He's with the DEA, Dante."

"What's his name?"

"Alex Whitehead."

Quiet a moment, thinking and trying to get his mind in correct order, Dante shifted his eyes back to Angela from the window just as the waitress walked up to their table.

After the waitress took their order, she shot Dante a smile to which Dante paid no attention before walking off. Angela noticed and was now mean-mugging the white woman. Dante spoke up, getting Angela's attention back on him. "Listen! I want you to get as much information on this Alex Whitehead guy as you can. Then let me know. I'ma deal with Whitehead Junior myself."

"I'll start on that as soon as I get back to the office, but I've got something else to tell you."

"What's up?"

"Do you remember the guy you asked me to have my people watch for you?" Angela asked, seeing Dante nod his head in response. "Well, I have information for you on this Raul Martinez guy. It's out in the car."

Nodding his head in response to what Angela just told him, Dante then said, "Look! After I handle this thing with Raul, I'ma leave town for a while to handle some business."

"What about what I just told you about Captain Whitehead's son?"

"Just have the information for me when I get back in town."

"How long are you gonna be gone for?"

"I'll let you know before I leave town," Dante told her, just as the waitress returned with their food smiling brightly while staring straight at Dantc.

* * *

Getting business for the day taken care of after dropping Harmony off at the spot where Tony T was supposed to meet up with her later, Alinna made it back to the house and parked the BMW in front of the house just as her cell phone went off.

Digging for the cell phone in her bag as she headed to the front door to the house, she saw that it was Amber once she touched the screen. Alinna answered the call as she was unlocking the front door, "Yeah! What's up, Amber?"

"Alinna, where the hell you at?"

Hearing the tone of Amber's voice and how rushed her words came out, Alinna locked the front door to the house once she was inside and responded, "Amber, I'm at the house. What the hell wrong with you, girl?"

"You ain't heard about Rick?"

"Heard what about Rick?" Alinna asked, as she headed upstairs. "What's up with Rick's ass anyway?"

"Alinna, he dead!"

Stopping where she was right before stepping off the steps onto the second level, Alinna asked, "Amber, what the hell is you talking about?"

Listening to Amber, her girl told her how she heard about Rick's body being found with a hole in the side of his head. Alinna made her way to her bedroom and then asked, "They found out who done killed 'em?"

"Nobody really knows, but word on the street is that some out-of-town niggas did it."

Dropping down onto her bed sighing loudly, Alinna had a pretty good idea who the out-of-town niggas was that killed Rick.

"What's up, Alinna?" Amber asked, speaking up. "You thinking it's who I'm thinking?"

"Pretty much," Alinna answered. "Look, Amber, let me call you back, alright?"

"Alright, girl."

Hanging up the phone and tossing it onto the bed beside her, Alinna sighed, pushed herself up from the bed, and headed towards the bathroom when her phone rang again.

Dismissing the call, Alinna continued to the bathroom, only to stop and back up in front of the closet where she noticed a white piece of paper and a gold key taped to the closet door.

Snatching up both the key and paper, Alinna unfolded the paper and read the note, which she quickly realized was from Dante. Balling up the note angrily after reading his bullshit, Alinna stepped into the closet and noticed that all of Dante's things were gone.

"Muthafucker!" Alinna said, marching back over to the bed, snatching up her cell phone, and calling Dante's ass.

Hearing the wireless customer, no longer had service, she realized he had cut off his phone. Alinna then looked up Vanessa's number and called her.

"Yeah, Alinna! What's up?"

"You wanna explain to me why the hell Dante left a message explaining that if I wanted to contact him concerning my son or business, I had to go through you?"

"Alinna, I spoke to Dante earlier and he told me that since you wanted to believe what you want, then he was done trying to stop you from believing it. I got him to agree to continue with doing business with us, and, yes, he's asked me to be his contact person."

"Oh, so you just done jump on his side now, huh?"

"I haven't jumped on anyone's side. I just think you're making a big mistake concerning Dante. Instead of kicking him out, you should have talked to him."

"What the fuck you think I been trying to do with his lying ass?"

"If you was doing what the hell you doing to me right now, then I'm surprised Dante ain't knock your ass out. You yelling for nothing."

"For nothing, huh?" Alinna yelled. "So me dealing with my man having a baby with some police bitch is nothing, huh? Or the fact that he still fucking this bitch, huh?"

"You don't know if Dante . . ."

"I followed his ass to the bitch Angela's house, Vanessa. I saw her kiss him and he allowed it."

"But did you see him fucking her?"

"You know what? Just from the way he stood there and let that bitch kiss him was enough to tell me everything I needed. She can have his ass!"

"That's gonna be your loss, Alinna."

"Whatever!" Alinna responded, sucking her teeth. "Just give me Dante's new number. I need to talk to him about what happened to Rick."

"I already told him. He knows."

"Wait!" Alinna said in disbelief. "You mean to tell me you called and told Dante our business before you called and made sure I knew what was going on?"

"I had Amber call and tell you."

"You know what? Whatever, Vanessa! Just give me Dante's new number. I know you got it!"

"He told me not to give it to you."

"What?" Alinna screamed. "You know what, Vanessa. Keep the fucking number!"

Alinna hung up on Vanessa and caught herself before throwing her cell phone across the room at the bedroom wall. Instead, she stood up, tossed the phone on the bed, and marched back towards the bathroom, slamming the door behind her.

* * *

Dante hooked up with both Dre and Tony T at his hotel room. He explained to his boys about the hit out in Phoenix of some major drug dealer, Victor Fayman. He went into what details he had, explaining that they were leaving in two days, on Friday afternoon.

Noticing Dre's mood, Dante decided to talk with his boy before he and Tony T left, walking both his boys out to their rides.

"Ay, yo, Dre!" Dante called out to the big man, as he was dapping up with Tony T.

Watching Dante walk over to him from Tony T's Aston Martin, Dre turned and faced his best friend . . . his brother.

"What's up, fam?" Dante asked, slapping five with his boy. "What's on ya mind kin folks?"

"You tell me!" Dre replied, before asking, "What's up with you and Alinna? Why you let her kick you out the house?"

Sighing deeply as he leaned against the side of Dre's SUV, Dante pulled out his box of Black & Mild's and said, "Family, look! I'll admit that I fucked up in the beginning by not telling

Alinna what was going on between me and Angela, even if she was putting the force game down on me. The problem is that Alinna can only see what's happening from her perspective and closing her eyes to the sacrifices I made that were meant for her. She don't see the bullets I'm barely getting away from just to give her what she wants. All she can see is that I fucked up!"

"So you just giving up then?"

"Naw!" Dante answered. "I promised I'd never give up on her, but I won't force her to stay if she don't want it. I still gotta son and a daughter I gotta take care of and as long as I'm breathing, I'ma make sure they want for nothing."

"It's just one thing though - family!" Dre said in a voice that caused Dante to shift his eyes over to him. He continued, "Them some bullets you keep ducking for this chick, fam. You just better make sure one never finds yo ass."

Hearing his boy but not bothering to reply, Dante had a quick thought and wondered if Alinna would even give a fuck whether he was shot and killed.

* * *

After leaving the hotel a little while after both Tony T and Dre were gone, Dante pushed his Ninja, driving across town to meet up with Wesley at one of his trap houses he ran out in Opa-Locka.

Pulling up to the trap a little while later and parking behind Wesley's Cadillac Escalade, Dante shut off the Ninja, climbed off the bike, and removed his bike helmet.

"De original gangsta is here!" Wesley yelled in an excited thick Jamaican accept. He walked up to meet Dante from where he stood on the front porch of the trap house with a few of his co-workers. "What go me, brethren?"

"What's up, Wesley?" Dante asked, embracing the Jamaican. He released him and asked, "You ready to put in some work, Rude Boy?"

"Who de blood clot boy is, me brethren? Me ready to dead dem now!" Wesley replied, smiling as he placed his right hand on the print of his burner that was under his shirt, stuck in the front of his jeans.

Dante broke down everything he had on Raul Martine, whom Wesley remembered. After explaining, Wesley asked, "When do we leave?"

"Now!" Dante replied.

Wesley turned back toward the house and yelled out to one of the workers on the porch to bring him out his toy.

A young-looking worker rushed back out of the house carrying a black leather duffel bag. Dante took the bag through the passenger door window and felt the weight. He recognized the feel of what was inside.

"Where de dead boy live?" Wesley asked as he pulled off from in front of the trap house.

* * *

They made it out to West Palm and easily found the high-rise apartment building, which was out near the beach. Wesley parked the Escalade across the street from the front of the 14-story apartment building. While Dante sat and watched the front door as women and men walked in and out of the building, he noticed the doorman at the front entrance.

"What go on?" Wesley asked, watching Dante and waiting.

Remaining quiet for a moment in thought, Dante continued staring out the window at the apartment entrance and then broke his silence, "Leave the duffel bag inside the truck. We won't need it. But follow me inside after five minutes, alright?"

Not waiting for a response, Dante climbed out of the Escalade and shut the truck door. He started across the street and walked to the front entrance where the doorman pushed the door open for him.

"Good afternoon, sir!" the doorman spoke.

Nodding his head to the doorman and glancing around the building's lobby, Dante turned to face the doorman, just as he was opening the front door for a couple.

Nodding a greeting to the couple as they passed him on their way to the elevator, Dante shifted his eyes over to the doorman, who turned to face him and asked, "Yes, sir! Can I help you with something?"

"I'm looking for what apartment either Gina Ortez or Raul Martinez is living in."

"Are they expecting you, sir?"

"No."

"Well then, sir, I'm sorry. I cannot help you," the doorman replied with a smile to Dante. However, as the doorman turned around when hearing the door open, he was met by a dark-skinned man pointing a black gun at him. "Oh, God!"

"We gonna try this again," Dante said calmly. "What apartment is Gina Ortez or Raul Martinez living in?"

This time Dante got a quick answer from the doorman and turned to walk off. He then called back to Wesley and, in patois, said, "Take care of the doorman and then meet me in apartment F-37."

He took the elevator to the sixth floor. Dante stepped off the elevator and took a moment to look at the apartment door numbers. He then turned right and headed up the hall.

When he arrived at apartment F-37, Dante knocked on the door and stood waiting a moment until he heard a soft female voice call out, "Yes! Who is it?"

"Gina Ortez?"

"Yes! Can I help you?"

"Yes, ma'am. There's been a…" He mumbled the rest.

"What did you say? I couldn't hear you that good. Can you repeat that?"

Dante again mumbled Raul's name and hospital in the same sentence. He then heard Gina ask him to hold on, as she unlocked the apartment door for him.

"What were you saying about Raul?" Gina asked, after opening the apartment door.

Meeting the woman's eyes, Dante started, "I was saying Raul should have been more careful."

Snatching his Glock from under his shirt faster than Gina could catch on to what was happening, Dante pressed the front of the gun against her forehead. Seeing her body stiffen, he calmly said, "Now understand. You scream and I'ma blow ya melon head in half. Nod if you understand."

Dante watched Shorty nod her head yes and then heard the ring of the elevator. He cut his eyes to his right, looking back up the hallway to see Wesley stepping off the elevator.

Pushing Gina back inside her apartment, he followed her in. Dante left the apartment door open as he walked her inside the front room. He had her sit on the white fur sofa.

"Where Raul?" Dante asked, looking around the nicely decorated apartment. He heard Wesley walk inside the apartment, close the door, and then lock it.

"Wh-who are you? What do you want?" Gina asked, looking first at the guy with the gold at the bottom of his mouth over to the dark-skinned guy who had just walked into the apartment.

Not bothering with answering Gina's questions, Dante spoke in patois, telling Wesley to check the apartment and make sure nobody else was inside.

Turning his attention back to Gina and meeting her eyes, Dante repeated his question again. "Where Raul?"

She stared at the guy in front of her a moment. He held his eyes on her. Gina finally answered, "He left to take care of something."

"How long ago he left?"

"Maybe a little over 30 minutes."

"Who was he with?"

"What's all this about?" Gina asked. "Who are you?"

"Everything clear," Wesley said in patois, as he entered back into the front room.

Acknowledging Wesley's statement with a simple head nod, Dante shifted his eyes back to Gina and said, "Listen! I don't like repeating myself and I've done it twice already. You now have two choices. You can either answer my question or I'll figure this out without you. Decide now!"

Staring quietly at the guy in front of her, understanding perfectly well the real meaning of his warning, Gina answered softly, "He's with two of his friends. They came to pick him up."

"He tell you where he was going?"

"No!" Gina answered. "He never tells me where he's going when he's handling his business."

Nodding his head in understanding, Dante looked over to the couch to his left, across from Gina, walked over, and sat down. "I guess we're about to sit here together and wait on your man to show up then."

* * *

Alinna walked out of the beauty salon after getting her hair washed and her nails done up in a French manicure. She headed towards her BMW just as her cell phone started ringing.

Digging out her phone from inside her Gucci bag, Alinna stopped at the driver's door to her car. She sucked her teeth when she saw that Vanessa was calling.

"What Vanessa?"

"Alinna, where you at?"

"Why?"

"Alinna, Harmony's been shooting with some niggas and she been shot. Tony T going crazy."

"What?" Alinna yelled. "What the fuck happen? Where the fuck Harmony at?"

"She at Parkway Hospital with Amber and Tony T. I'm about to call Dante now."

"What happen exactly? Who shot Harmony?" Alinna asked, as she was rushing to unlock her car door.

"From what Amber said, Tony T told her it was some of Raul's boys again."

"Shit!" Alinna cursed, punching the steering wheel. "Listen, I'm on my way to Parkway now. Meet me there."

"I'm already heading there now. I'ma see you when you get there."

"Yeah!" Alinna replied, hanging up the phone and tossing it over into the passenger seat with her handbag. She punched the steering wheel again. "Shit! Shit! Shit!"

* * *

Dante hung up his phone after talking with Vanessa about Harmony. He then looked at Wesley and, in patois, explained about Harmony and what Vanessa said went down with some of Raul's men and that she was now at Parkway Hospital.

"What happened?" Gina asked, staring between the two men and seeing the expression on their faces.

Shifting his eyes over toward Gina, Dante stared a few moments and finally answered, "It seems like Raul has been really busy."

"Wh-what's happened?" Gina repeated the question, as she began to cry. She stared at the guy seated across from her who was now texting on his cell phone.

He ignored Gina as he continued texting with Vanessa, letting her know that he and Wesley would be over to the hospital after they were finished handling a little business. Dante sent the text message to Vanessa just as he heard a phone ring nearby.

Dante looked in the direction of the kitchen and saw Wesley walking towards the breakfast bar, where a pink cell phone lay. Dante met the dread's dark eyes when Wesley turned facing him with a half-smile.

"Da blood clot boy is calling," Wesley told Dante in broken English, as he made his way back over into the front room and stood beside the couch next to Dante. He handed him the phone while staring at Gina.

Dante took the cell phone from Wesley and glanced down at the screen to see Raul's name. He tossed the touch screen across to Gina, watching her catch the phone with a confused and surprised look on her face.

"Call 'em back after the phone stops ringing," Dante told her. "Let 'em know you taking care of something and couldn't stop to answer the phone."

Gina stared at the guy with the golds. Once the cell phone stopped ringing, she took a deep breath and then did as she told and called Raul back.

"Yeah!" Raul answered on the second ring.

Speaking in Spanish, Gina was only able to get out a few words when the guy across from her held up his gun and pointed at her.

"English!" Dante told her.

"Who the fuck is that?" Gina heard Raul ask angrily, as she sat staring across from her at the guy with the gold in his mouth.

17

"Raul, what do you want?" Gina asked, while still staring at the gunman. "I'm in the middle of doing something."

"Doing what?" Raul yelled. "What the fuck are you doing, Gina? Who the fuck there with you?"

"Hang up the phone," Dante told her, loud enough to be heard over the phone.

Doing what she was told, Gina hung up the phone as tears ran heavily down her face.

Ignoring the tears, Dante shifted his eyes to Wesley who stood behind Gina. He nodded his head slightly and then sat and watched Wesley pull out a long black-handled machete from the side of his jeans. With one heavy swing to Gina's neck, Dante watched the woman's head fly off, hitting the toss pillow on the sofa beside the now headless body.

3

Raul Martinez was angrily talking to himself in Spanish as he and his boys stepped off the elevator on the floor of his apartment building. He marched down the hallway to his apartment, keys in hand.

Arriving at his apartment, he unlocked the door and forcefully pushed it open. Raul stepped into the room, yelling out for Gina.

"Gina, where the fuck …? Oh, God. No!" Raul cried, seeing his lady sitting on the sofa. He was unable to understand how her head was sitting on the coffee table in front of her and staring at him.

"Looks like she not happy to see you."

Raul swung around and was surprised by what he saw.

It took him a moment to understand what was taking place. Both his boys lay face down, while a dark-skinned guy stood over them holding a banger. He then shifted his eyes over to the light-skinned guy who was seated at the breakfast bar, pointing a burner at him.

Raul then asked, "Who the…who the fuck is you?"

"I'm surprised you don't know," Dante replied, as he sat calmly across the room staring at Raul. "I'll help you out though. You seem to have a little problem with a friend of mine. Name's Harmony and runs a spot 'cross over in Miami. You know who I'm talking about, don't you?"

"How much she paying you?" Raul asked, ignoring Dante's question. "I'll pay you $80,000 to change your mind if you take your boy and leave."

"$80,000 not enough, Raul," Dante replied. "Make it $100,000 and I'll think about it."

"That's no problem," Raul told him. "I got the money inside the safe in my bedroom. You can have it."

Nodding his head slowly, Dante climbed from his high chair and nodded toward the hallway leading to the bedroom. "Lead the way!"

They followed Raul to the back of the apartment and into his nicely furnished bedroom. Dante stood at the foot of the bed as Raul opened the closet, stepped inside, and bent down reaching for something.

Dante was holding a Glock in each hand as Raul returned from the closet carrying a mid-size safe. He saw the surprised look on Raul's face upon seeing both bangers in his hands.

"Just open the safe, Raul."

Doing as he was told, Raul used the key he had tied onto the side of the safe. He then opened the door and looked over at Dante.

"I offered and you agreed to $100,000," Raul stated, as he stared at Dante.

"I tell you what," Dante told him, nodding his head over to the window. "Stand over there."

"Man, you can relax."

"I don't like repeating myself, Raul," Dante told him, staring a moment until Raul moved over and stood in front of the window.

Dante walked over to the safe and looked inside, seeing the chrome .25 automatic taped to the inside of the safe's walls. He smirked and looked over at Raul. Then he focused on the money inside the safe.

"Alright, Raul," Dante said, looking toward Raul who was staring back at him. "I ain't gonna kill you."

"What you gonna do with me...?"

Dante spoke up again, cutting off Raul. "Since I promised not to kill you, I want you to open up the window behind you and jump out of it."

Dante watched the expression on Raul's face and then said, "You can either die that way or die like your lady did. Either way, yo ass gonna die today. Decide now!"

* * *

Alinna stood at Harmony's bedside at Parkway Hospital, watching her girl sleeping after being given drugs for the pain. She turned around to see Tony T walk into the room, followed by Vanessa, Dre, and Amber.

Following Tony T with her eyes as he walked over to Harmony's beside and seeing the expression on his face as he bent down and kissed Harmony's soft lips, Alinna looked back over her shoulder at hearing Amber ask, "How the doctor say she doing, Alinna?"

"She'll be okay!" Alinna told her girl, turning to face Amber and Vanessa while ignoring the look on Dre's face as he stood staring down at her. She continued, "They was able to get the bullet out but they're watching to make sure no infection or anything else pops up."

"What about Raul?" Amber asked. "What are we gonna do about his ass?"

"Dante said he was dealing with Raul," Vanessa told Amber only for Alinna to speak up angrily, "You know what, Vanessa? I really am getting tired of you and Dante's this and that. It's amazing how you all of a sudden got all this fucking faith in his lying ass."

"You know what bi . . ."

"Andre!" Vanessa said, shooting Dre a look before grabbing Alinna and dragging her out of the hospital room into the hallway.

"Look! If you about to tell me about . . ."

"You know what, Alinna!" Vanessa said, cutting Alinna off, "You keep talking about how sorry and how much of a lie Dante is but if it wasn't for him, you wouldn't be where you are right now. Matter of fact, none of us would be where we are if Dante wasn't out there risking his life doing what he's doing. I know he messed up with Angela and he knows it but there's no doubt that Dante loves your ass, Alinna."

"Fuck Dante!" Alinna said angrily.

"Speaking of Dante," Amber said, as she and Dre stood behind both Vanessa and Alinna nodding her head up the hallway. "Look who's coming this way now!"

Turning and looking to see who Amber was talking about, Alinna froze as she watched Dante walking her way, barely noticing Wesley walking next to him.

Dante simply walked right passed Alinna and up to Vanessa as Alinna just stared. Vanessa hugged Dante's neck. When Alinna saw him kiss Vanessa's cheek and return her hug, she felt her anger skyrocket at being disrespected.

"What's up, big bruh?" Vanessa said, smiling up at Dante.

"Everything good, lil sis?" Dante answered, as he released Vanessa. He then embraced Amber and dapped up with his boy Dre. "So, what's up with my girl, Harmony? How she doing?"

"If you wasn't out running behind the next bitch, you would know," Alinna said, watching Dante cut his eyes back at her.

"Come on, Dante!" Vanessa said, grabbing his hand and shooting Alinna a nasty look. "Let's go see Harmony."

Sucking her teeth as she watched Vanessa lead Dante into Harmony's hospital room, Alinna ignored the look that Dre shot her as she followed Amber into the room.

Once inside the hospital room, both Tony T and Dante embraced each other while Wesley and Tony T dapped. Vanessa explained to Dante what the doctor had said about Harmony's health. Dante stood affectionately rubbing the side of Harmony's face.

"She wouldn't be lying there if you would have taken care of Raul like you said you would and not chase behind that bitch, Angela," Alinna said nastily, causing everybody in the room to stare at her.

"Alinna, you know what . . ."

"Naw!" Dante spoke up, cutting off Vanessa as he stood staring at Alinna. "She right. I should have handled Raul when I said I would but I can't change what's already happened. I know it'll never happen again, though. That's my word."

"Your word ain't shit, nigga!" Alinna told him.

"Vanessa!" Amber cried, stepping towards her girl, who was moving towards Alinna.

"Oh! So what, you gonna fight me over Dante now, Vanessa?" Alinna asked, staring at Vanessa in surprise.

"Look!" Amber spoke up again. "What we need to figure out is how we gonna be able to deal with Raul ass. Y'all not fighting each other."

"De blood clot boy no problem no more," Wesley spoke up, drawing everyone's attention to him.

"How you figure that, baby?" Amber asked her man.

"Me brethren killed the rude boy," Wesley answered, smiling over at Dante.

"Wait a minute!" Amber said, looking to Dante. "When you kill Raul, Dante?"

"Wesley!" Dante called out to the dread. "Turn on the news."

"What's going on, fam?" Dre asked Dante, as Wesley turned on the television.

Dante nodded his head toward the TV, as Channel 7 News reported a possible homicide turned suicide at the West Palm High Rise apartment building, leaving three bodies found dead inside an apartment rented out to a Gina Ortez. Dante then waited until the news reporter said Raul Martinez's name as among the deceased. He then looked at Alinna asking, "You happy now?"

Alinna looked from the television to Dante's eyes, as he stood staring at her. However, she never got the chance to respond as Dante turned to Vanessa and asked to speak with her for a few minutes.

Alinna watched both Vanessa and Dante leave the room into the hallway. She looked at Dre who asked, "You still got some fucked up shit to say about my brother or is you happy now?"

* * *

"What's up, big bruh?" Vanessa asked, as she and Dante walked up the hallway.

"I need you to promise me something, Nessa," Dante told her, turning his head and looking at her.

"What's up, Dante? Just ask it." Vanessa told him, taking his hand inside hers as they walked side by side.

Stopping in front of the elevator, and turning to face Vanessa, Dante said, "Look, lil sis. I really don't wanna keep dealing with Alinna and the bullshit but I need you to take D.J. over to see his sister, Mya, at Angela's place. She already knows you're going to be coming by."

"You serious, Dante?"

"Yeah!"

"Wait a minute!" Vanessa said, gripping Dante's hand tighter. "Why can't you take D.J. to see his sister?"

"I told you before that I leaving town soon, Nessa."

"But you coming back, right?"

Slowly smiling as he reached out and brushed Vanessa's hair back from her face, Dante said, "I'll always come if you need me, baby sis. Just promise me you got me on this."

Nodding her head, Vanessa accepted the kiss to the forehead from Dante and then stood watching him turn and walk onto the elevator just as two nurses were stepping off. She smiled as she watched both nurses nearly break their necks turning back to check out Dante before the elevator door closed shut.

Shaking her head as she turned around, Vanessa started walking back towards Harmony's room. She started to wonder how she had allowed herself to develop feelings and allow Dante into her heart when at first she couldn't stand his ass.

When Vanessa walked back in Harmony's hospital room the others were having a discussion. She stepped over beside Dre and leaned into his side only to hear Alinna ask, "Where the hell Dante ass at?"

Rolling her eyes, Vanessa answered, "Dante left, Alinna. He went to handle something."

"Handle what?"

"His business, Alinna. Damn!" Vanessa answered with an attitude. She continued, "Also, I'm taking my nephew and A.J. out this weekend to spend time with them. Do you have a problem with that?"

"Whatever, Vanessa!" Alinna replied, rolling her eyes at her. She turned back to the others and they continued their discussion.

* * *

After the issue resolved with Raul Martinez, Dante spent the next two days getting things ready for the trip that he, Tony T, and Dre were making to Phoenix. He wanted to out things with the nigga Victor Fayman who was pushing some major weight in Arizona.

Dante was surprised to see Vanessa climbing out of the front passenger seat with his son in her arms. He allowed a small smile to show as he stood and watched Vanessa walk up the yard and onto the porch in front of him.

"Hey, big bruh!" Vanessa said, as she leaned into Dante, wrapping her free left arm around his neck and kissing him while they hugged.

"What's up, lil sis?" Dante replied, taking his son from Vanessa once she released him. "Why didn't you tell me you was coming with Dre and Tony T?"

"Because it wasn't planned," Vanessa answered, smiling as she stood watching Dante playing with both his kids. It was only the second time she saw him smile since she had known him. "I just found out that you, Dre, and Tony T were leaving for Arizona from here. I figured this was a good time to really get to meet this Angela chick who Alinna hates so much."

Dante didn't respond. Instead, he turned a little towards the front door and tapped loudly so Angela could hear from inside the house. Dante then kissed both his kids foreheads.

Turning his attention back to the front of the house, he saw both Dre and Tony T packing bags inside the Ford Explorer they had rented under a false name. Dante looked back over his shoulder as he saw Angela step out of the doorway.

"Hey, Papi! What's the ...who is she?" Angela asked, after noticing the tall woman on her front porch.

"Angela. This my sister, Vanessa!" He then introduced Angela to Vanessa as Mya's mother.

"So, you're the Angela I've been hearing about, huh?" Vanessa said, looking over the baby mother of her brother's daughter. She was surprised at how pretty the female was but then she thought about how pretty Alinna was and how good Dante was always looking which made her realize she really wasn't all that surprised.

"Vanessa Green!" Angela said, looking Vanessa over slowly. "I recognized the name."

"You would since you a detective now. A new captain with the help of my brother," Vanessa replied with a slight attitude. She looked at Dante after hearing him say her name, meeting his eyes as he stared at her over the head of his son.

Sighing deeply, Vanessa looked back at Angela and apologized, "Sorry! I'm not used to dealing with the police."

"It's okay!" Angela replied. "You can relax. I'm on your side, Vanessa."

"That's what Dante tells me," Vanessa said in response, just as both Dre and Tony T walked up.

"Hi, Andre," Angela spoke, smiling at Dre.

"What's up, Angela?" Dre asked, nodding his head at Angela as he caught the look Vanessa shot back at him over her shoulder.

"What's up, fellas? We ready?" Dante asked as he handed Vanessa his daughter and then gave D.J. over to Angela.

We good, Play Boy?" Tony T answered, pulling his cell phone out and staring down at the screen.

Dante turned to Angela and kissed her on the lips and his son's head. Then he kissed Vanessa's cheek and the top of Mya's head before walking off. Both Dre and Tony T followed behind him.

Dante climbed inside the passenger front seat of the Ford Explorer, as Tony T climbed inside the back seat. Dre walked around to the driver's seat. Dante glanced out the window, seeing both Vanessa and Angela stepping inside the house as Dre began asking about Victor Fayman.

"It's a lil party that's supposed to be jumping off at some night club named Royalty," Dante told Dre. Pulling out his Black & Mild's, he continued, "From what I found out, this clown Victor supposed to be having his 30th birthday party at this club."

"When this party supposed to be?" Dre asked, glancing over to Dante from the road.

"We should get to Phoenix by Thursday and the party supposed to be Saturday night," Dante answered. He looked back at hearing Tony T call his name.

"Harmony wanna talk to you, bruh!" Tony T told him, handing Dante his cell phone.

Taking the phone, Dante turned back facing front. He placed the phone to his ear and said, "Yeah! What's up, Harmony?"

"Hey, boo!" Harmony happily said after hearing Dante's voice. "I just wanted to tell you thanks for the money you left me. Where you get a hundred grand from, boy?"

"Let's just say it's an apology for not handling that lil problem when I was supposed to."

"Tony T told me what you did. Thanks, Dante."

"No, thank you! We family."

"I love you, boy."

"Yeah! Love you too, Harmony," Dante told her, passing the phone back to Tony T.

Watching his boy while driving the rental, Dre easily noticed the change in his best friend. He also noticed the way that Dante was opening himself up to feel for the others inside the family and Angela since having both his son, D.J., and his daughter, Mya.

"What's up, family?" Dante asked, while noticing Dre watching him.

Smiling, Dre answered, "Nothing, fam! It ain't nothing, bruh!"

4

Finishing up business for the day after making her last sale, Alinna drove her BMW home while trying to ignore the thoughts of Dante she had been having all day. She was unwilling to admit she actually missed him after not seeing him since Harmony was shot by Raul's people.

Deep in thought about Dante, she heard a bell-like sound inside her car. Glancing down to see the gas light was on, Alinna cursed and, after looking back at the road, noticed she was passing a BP gas station.

Making a quick left turn, Alinna pulled into the gas station entrance just as a metallic gray Cadillac ATS-V was pulling out of the gas station. She slammed on the brakes too late and ran into the ATS.

"Shit!" Alinna cursed, throwing the BMW into park before jumping out of the car. A tall, clean-shaven, brown-skinned guy climbed out of the ATS yelling, "Muthafucker! What the fuck is wrong with you? Can't you read?"

Looking at the exit sign that shorty was pointing at, the guy looked back to the short but sexy-as-hell female. He slowly smiled and said, "I read pretty good, beautiful. But you may wanna look at the sign again though."

"What?" Alinna replied, seeing homeboy nodding his head. She looking over at the entrance sign only to freeze at realizing the sign actually said exit. "Shit!"

Smiling still as he slowly looked the female over, he said, "Relax, gorgeous! It was an accident. I'm willing to forget about it if you'll do two things for me."

Looking the guy over in his Ralph Lauren navy-blue suit that showed off his nicely muscular body, Alinna noticed the smile on his face. She shook her head wondering where things were about to go. "What exactly is it you want…?"

"Alex!" he finished for Alinna. He then asked, "I was only wondering what your name was? And would you consider having dinner with me this weekend?"

Sighing loudly, Alinna started to reply, only for Alex to speak up again, "I'm not asking for anything more than your name and dinner. Nothing more and nothing less."

Staring at the guy a moment, Alinna noticed that he was actually cute. She sighed again and said, "My name's Alinna, Alex."

Smiling a little more as he walked closer, he held out his hand to Alinna and said, "It's good meeting you, Alinna. I hope this also means you'll have dinner with me tomorrow night."

Staring up into his eyes and ignoring the thought of Dante, Alinna heard herself say, "Alright, Alex! We can have dinner this one time."

* * *

Making it to the house later than she had planned, after talking with the cutie Alex at the BP station, Alinna parked the BMW in the front of the house and headed to the front door. Just then, the door swung open and Vanessa stepped out with D.J. in her arms.

"Where you two going?" Alinna asked Vanessa. She then bent over and kissed D.J.'s cheek, which caused him to smile at her.

"I'm taking my nephew out to eat dinner. Just him and his auntie."

"What about A.J.?"

"He's already asleep in Rose's room. He and me got plans tomorrow," Vanessa told her. She continued, "Yeah! I talked to Dante, too. They made it to Phoenix and should be hooking up with this Victor guy tomorrow night. He said they should be back by Monday if everything goes right."

"Whatever!" Alinna replied carelessly, rolling her eyes as she walked past Vanessa into the house.

Shaking her head, Vanessa walked out to her BMW truck and put D.J. inside A.J.'s baby seat in the back. Then she climbed up front behind the wheel.

Pulling out her cell phone, Vanessa called Angela's phone as she was cranking up the truck.

"Hello!" Angela answered after two rings.

"Angela, you home yet? This Vanessa."

"I walked into the house just now. You still coming over?"

"I'm on my way over with D.J. now."

"Okay! We'll be ready when you get here. Have you talked to Dante yet?"

"He hasn't called you yet?"

"Dante doesn't like to call me when he's out of town."

"Well, Dante's fine and he says they should be back by Monday."

"That's good to hear. But the next time you talk to him, let him know I got the information he wanted before he left."

"What information?"

"I'll let Dante tell you that when you talk to him."

"Well, let me get off this phone. I'll be to the house in a little while."

After hanging up with Angela, Vanessa continued driving but wondered what Angela was talking about and what Dante was up to.

* * *

Finding out a little more information about Victor Fayman while trailing the guy all over Phoenix, Dante found out that he was already dealing with a little issue with some Dominican cocaine dealer who actually had Phoenix in a chokehold. That is, until Victor had shown up, stepping on the feet of the Dominican and stealing business away from him.

Dante was dressed in an all-black Sean John suit with a matching button-up dress shirt, no tie, and Sean John shoes. Dante was waiting outside next to the Ford Explorer, which was parked inside the hotel parking lot where they were staying. He turned and saw Dre and Tony T finally step out of the hotel dressed up as well.

"I ain't feeling all this suit-wearing shit!" Dre said, as he headed towards the driver's door, shooting Dante a look.

Climbing inside the front passenger seat, Dante looked over to Dre and said, "Relax, family. It's just for tonight. Once we handle this clown Victor, we outta here and heading back home."

Once Dre cranked up the Explorer and pulled out of the hotel parking lot, Dante went over the plan again with both Tony T and Dre, as they headed towards Club Royalty where Victor's birthday party was being celebrated.

They arrived 20 minutes later to a long-as-hell line of cars, SUVs, and hooked-up trucks. Dante sat smoking a Black while staring out his window as Dre slowly made his way up the road, seeing females and groups of different guys walking up the road heading to the nightclub.

After Dre found a spot to park a short ways from the club, Dante, Dre, and Tony T walked back up towards the club. They received a few calls from the ladies in line, which they ignored, as they continued on with their business.

"I see homeboy got a lil style," Tony T said, nodding to the two stretch Mercedes truck limos.

Dante noticed the limos but paid no attention to them, as he, Dre, and Tony T walked through the club's front parking area. He called out to Dre and watched his boy step ahead of him, forcefully pushing open a path through the thick crowd that was blocking their way to the front door of the club. Tony T stepped ahead up to three security dudes who were blocking the doors to the club.

He spoke with the security guards while Dante stood behind and, still smoking his Black, watched Tony T hand each of the security guards some money. Tony T then nodded back at him and Dre.

They received nods from two of the guards, so Dante and Dre started moving forward to enter the nightclub. However, Dante was stopped and grabbed by the third security on the right.

"Put out the cigar before you enter the club," the third security guard told Dante, staring hard at him.

Looking from the hand on his arm up to meet the brown eyes of the security guard, Dante calmly knocked the lit tip of the Black & Mild out of his mouth with his thumb. He looked at the security guard who then released him.

Shaking his head as he stepped through the doors of Club Royalty, Dante fell in step with both Tony T and Dre, slowly nodding his head to Jay-Z, Kanye West, and Big Sean's song "Click" that was banging from the club's speakers.

"Damn, baby! Who you?" a light-skinned female yelled over the music, stopping in front of Dante, blocking his path and smiling in his face.

Barely meeting the girls eyes, Dante stepped around her and continued in his direction to the bar, leaving the girl staring at him with her face balled up in both embarrassment and anger.

Making it to the bar, Dante directed his attention to the V.I.P. area easily spotting Victor Fayman as he stood with four girls surrounding him while huge crowds gathered around drinking and having a good time.

"For someone beefing with a muthafucker, homeboy hanging the fuck out, ain't he?" Tony T said. He moved beside Dante on his left side and handed his boy a bottle of Corona while also staring at the V.I.P. area.

"Naw!" Dante replied, as he took the bottle from Tony T. "Dude on point. He got six niggas with bangers up in V.I.P. with 'em, and I see three of his boys posted at the stairs while he up there. Homeboy at the door one of his, too."

"You mean the dude who stopped you about the Black?"

"Yeah! I saw him with Victor once before."

"So what's the plan on getting up there with this clown?" Dre yelled over the D.J., who was giving shout-outs to the birthday boy. Spotlights lit up the V.I.P. section.

Not answering Dre directly back, Dante took a sip of Corona and simply stared towards the V.I.P. section.

* * *

Dominic's chauffeur-driven pearl-white Bentley Continental GT pulled up in front of Club Royalty behind the Range Rover that had seven of his men inside. Another Range Rover followed behind. He stared angrily through his window as his driver followed the lead Range Rover through the parking lot of Club Royalty, seeing people quickly rush to get out of the way.

The Bentley stopped at the front of the club's entrance, as Dominic's men rushed out of both Range Rovers. Dominic waited until his armed driver opened his door for him. He climbed out of the Bentley as his head-of-security stepped up to meet him.

"Everyone's ready, sir," Carlos told his boss.

Nodding his head in response, while watching his men push through the crowd, Dominic spoke up saying, "Let's get this handled, Carlos."

* * *

"What's going on, Dre?" Tony T asked, watching Victor and his team rushing down the stairs from the V.I.P. area.

Noticing the same thing that Tony T was seeing, Dante looked over from Victor and his crew to the doors of the club's entrance, instantly recognizing the Dominican drug lord and the team he had with him as they rushed into the club.

"Shit about to get real as fuck up in this shit, fam!" Dre said, as he too stood watching the scene unfold.

As they were watching both crews meet head up, Dante came up with a plan. "Follow my lead, fellas! We about to make some shit happen."

* * *

"You must really be a stupid muthafucker coming up in here like you ready for war," Victor told Dominic, smirking at the Dominican.

"I'm glad to see this is a funny matter to you, Victor," Dominic replied, before adding, "The problem here though is that only one of us will leave this club tonight."

"You're right!" Victor said, smiling, just as a gun was placed up to the side of Dominic's head.

Dominic's security realized what was happening, so they pulled out their guns and turned towards their boss. Victor opened his mouth to say something when the bodyguard on his right went down, followed by the bodyguard on his left. He then felt a gun against the side of his head.

"Tell your man to put the gun down and then walk over this way," Dante told Victor as he held homeboy at gunpoint.

"You must not know who . . ."

Dante smashed the handle of his banger across the side of Victor's head. When Victor staggered to his left from the blow, Dante said again, "Tell ya men to put down their guns and walk this way."

Blinking his eyes to get his vision back after being hit across the head, Victor opened his mouth to say something to the gunman, only to feel the gun pressed harder against his head. He thought better of his decision and did what was told of him.

From the front door, Dante watched homeboy drop his gun from Dominic's head and lay the banger onto the ground. He waited until homeboy walked over and then released Victor, whispering, "This ain't finished between us."

Dre and Tony T followed Dante as they walked away from Victor and his team, still pointing their heaters at them. Dante stopped in front of Dominic and met the Dominican's eyes. He stepped around the man and walked through his crew towards the doors.

* * *

Once outside, Dante, Dre and Tony T ignored the stares as the three of them left the club and headed to their Ford Explorer.

"Fam, you plan on telling us what the fuck that was just now?" Dre asked, once the three of them were inside the SUV.

Dante didn't answer Dre and ignored Tony T staring at him from the back seat. He simply stared out the passenger window as Dre drove away. Dante wondered if he had made the right decision in helping the Dominican and not just dumping on the nigga Victor right there in the club.

"Yo!" Tony T called out from the back seat. "We got company, y'all!"

Looking back behind him through the black-tinted window, Dante saw the Range Rover, Bentley, and a second Range Rover drive past the Explorer. They pulled in front of them and blocked the middle of the road.

"Here we go!" Tony T said, pulling his hammer from under his black button-up.

"Relax!" Dante told Tony T and Dre. He then stared at the Bentley as the back door was opened and Dominic climbed out, with his team from the first Range Rover crowding around him. The rest of the team posted themselves in the middle of the road.

"Look at this shit!" Dre said, shaking his head. "It's this same Spanish muthafucker we just helped out."

Listening to Dre while watching one of the Dominican's men walk over to the driver's side, Dante told Dre to roll down the window. After a quick stare, Dre did as he was told.

"You!" Carlos said, nodding to Dante inside the passenger seat. "Mr. Saldana would like you to talk with him a moment."

"About what?" Dante asked, staring back at the homeboy outside of Dre's window.

"Mr. Saldana will discuss everything with you once you two are seated," Carlos answered, before asking Dante to please come with him.

"Yo, Dre! What's up?" Tony T asked, leaning forward between the front seats. "Bruh, you not really going to holla at this dude, is you?"

"I'ma be right back," Dante told his boys. He climbed out, closing the door behind him.

He walked around the front of the Explorer where the messenger was waiting. Dante allowed homeboy to pat him down, finding both his hammers.

"You will receive these back before you leave," Carlos told him. "Follow me, sir."

Following a step behind the messenger, while ignoring the hard-staring crew who were watching him closely, Dante stopped once face to face with the Dominican drug lord.

"Who, may I ask, are you?" Dominic asked, as he stared straight into the younger man's eyes.

"Your messenger said you wanted to talk. I'm listening," Dante told the drug lord, disregarding the question that was asked.

Nodding his head slowly, but never breaking eye contact with the young man in front of him, Dominic called to his head of security. He then said to Dante, "Sit with me. Let's talk."

Dante climbed into the back of the Bentley behind Dominic. The messenger shut the door behind them. Dante looked over at Dominic as he introduced himself. "I am Dominic Saldana. It is clear that you are not from here. I wonder why you would interfere with matters you know nothing about."

"A simple 'thank you' would do."

Smiling, as he stared at the younger man beside him, Dominic said, "You are correct. I do owe you my thanks, and I do thank you. But again, exactly why would you interfere with matters that are of no concern to you?"

"Maybe I just saw that your security wasn't handling your business, so I decided to help out."

"Why do I feel as if that is only part of the truth? Who are you?"

"You seem pretty interested in knowing who I am."

"I'm always interested in those who are new in town and just show up and interfere in matters, especially with the end result of saving my life. That is why I have a security team. So again I ask, 'Who are you?'"

Deciding to answer the Dominican's questions, Dante replied, "Dante. Dante Blackwell."

"Well, Mr. Blackwell. What brings you to Arizona? And as most out-of-towners normally reply, I ask that you not answer that you are just passing through. You and I both know that is not the case. Let's both start things off with honesty, Mr. Blackwell."

5

Dominic didn't realize how long they had been talking but he did find out about Dante's plan to rob Victor Fayman. They also discussed the problem between Victor and the Dominican mafia. Dominic then got Dante to open up as much as the young man was willing about his family back home in Miami, along with his two brothers in the Explorer, that were all in the same business he was in. But since there was no actually connect, he and his brothers did all the supplying for the family.

Interrupting Dante, Dominic asked, "So tell me, Dante. How long have you and your brothers been in this line of business of robbing for your family?"

"Well, I been at it since I was 15, but things with the family been going on almost a year now."

"And how has that been going?"

"It's good but could be better."

Nodding his head, Dominic said after a moment, "Dante...look! I am willing to make a deal with you but I want something from you in return."

"I'm listening."

"Okay! I'm willing to supply your family with all the cocaine they can handle. I also have a friend who owes me a favor. This friend is a major marijuana dealer and if that is of interest as well, I will arrange it so that your family will also be supplied with all the marijuana they can handle."

"What is it you want from me in return?"

"Your help," Dominic answered. "I will pay you to be my personal bodyguard. I will also pay you $1,000,000 after you have taken care of Victor Fayman permanently."

Slowly nodding his head after hearing Dominic's offer, Dante held the Dominican drug lord's eyes a few moments and finally said, "How about you let me think about this offer and I'll get back to you."

"Very well, Dante!" Dominic answered. He then added, "But I expect to have an answer from you tomorrow at 12 o'clock noon."

Calling out to Carlos, Dominic waited until the car door was opened and then told his head of security to return Dante's cell phone. He then turned to Dante and said, "I will see you tomorrow, Mr. Blackwell."

* * *

Returning to the house later than she had planned on, Vanessa carried a sleeping D.J. inside the house. She locked the door behind her and then headed upstairs to put her nephew to bed.

She walked up to Alinna's bedroom, only to find it empty. Vanessa left the empty room with D.J. and headed to her and Dre's bedroom. She laid D.J. down on her bed, took off his clothes, and covered him up.

Vanessa pulled out her cell phone as she was leaving the bedroom. She called Alinna's phone but it sent her straight to voice mail.

She hung up the phone as she stopped in front of Rose's bedroom, only to see the maid and A.J. both asleep on the maid's bed. Vanessa decided to leave her son asleep with Rose. Just when she was closing the maid's bedroom door, her cell phone rang in her hand.

Expecting to see Alinna's name on the screen, Vanessa broke out in a smile after seeing it was Dante calling. "Hey, big bruh. What's up with you?"

"What's up, lil sis? Where you at?"

"I'm at the house. What's wrong? You sound a little funny."

"I need to holla at you about something, sis."

"Hold on a second, Dante!" Vanessa told him, as she entered her bedroom.

Undressing down to her panties and leaving on the t-shirt she was wearing, Vanessa climbed into the bed next to her nephew. She placed the phone back up to her ear and said, "Yeah, Dante. What's wrong, big bruh?"

Vanessa listened as Dante told her about the offer he received from a connect where he and both Dre and Tony T were getting into details. Dante then explained what was being expected of him in return. Vanessa's mouth dropped wide open after hearing the amount of money he was being paid to be a bodyguard and the $1,000,000 he'd receive after dealing with a problem for the connect.

"So, what are you going to do?" Vanessa asked once Dante had finished. "How long do you have to stay op there? Can you come home?"

"Yeah, I can come home but if I agree to stay up here for this job, you and the others will be good. Y'all can finally have the connect y'all wanted."

"I think you need to talk to Alinna. Hold on!" Vanessa told him.

She clicked over the line and then called Alinna's phone again, clicking back over to Dante once the line started to ring. "Dante. You still there?"

"Yeah!" Dante answered, hearing the ringing. "Vanessa, who you calling?"

"Hello!" Alinna answered, laughing.

"Alinna, it's me, Vanessa. Where you at? I need to talk to you about something important."

"Vanessa, I'm kind of in the middle of something right now. Can't this wait until I get home?"

"It's about Dante and business."

Sucking her teeth, Alinna told Vanessa to hold on.

"Dante, you still there?" Vanessa asked.

"Yeah!" Dante responded.

"Hello! Vanessa, you there?" Alinna asked, coming back on the line.

"Yeah. I'm right here, girl."

"Well, hurry up and talk. I'm out with Alex and you're interrupting."

"Alex? Who's Alex?"

"Girl, this sexy-ass guy I met earlier today. He asked me out to dinner and we just left the movies," Alinna explained. "I'll tell you more tonight. Just hurry up and tell me what's so important."

Quiet a moment until Alinna called out her name, Vanessa answered, "Yeah, I'm here."

"So, you gonna tell me what's up or what?"

"Look, Alinna. I talked to Dante and he says that he's found us a connect but the problem is that he gonna have to stay in Arizona for a while. But the deal with the connect is only if Dante stays and becomes his personal bodyguard and takes care of a problem the connect is having."

"Okay. Why are you telling me this?"

"Alinna, you not serious? This Dante we're talking about."

"Fuck Dante! He can stay his ass wherever he at. I don't give a fuck what he does. But if he's getting us connected then tell his ass to go right the hell ahead and do it."

"Thanks for the go-ahead."

Quiet for a second, Alinna called to Vanessa asking her, "Who the fuck was that Vanessa?"

Shaking her head even though Alinna couldn't see her, Vanessa said, "It don't even matter, Alinna."

"I know you just didn't set me up like that. That better not be Dante that's on the phone."

"Yeah, it was Dante. But he's hung up now, though."

"Bitch, what the fuck was . . ."

"Don't even try it, Alinna!" Vanessa cut her off. "How you gonna sit there acting like you all mad after all that shit you was just talking about Dante. He called to talk to us about this deal he was just offered and to see how we felt about it but you in the street up in some nigga face. Don't worry about it, though. You just helped Dante make his decision to stay in Arizona. Thank yourself, Alinna."

Vanessa angrily hung up the phone while Alinna was still running her mouth. She still couldn't believe what she just heard Alinna saying about Dante. And to make it worse, she was out with some other nigga.

"Fuck her!" Vanessa said out loud to herself, still thinking about how Alinna was talking shit about Dante. "She wanna fuck with some nobody, that's her business. I just hope my big brother finds something better where he at."

* * *

Dante stood at his hotel room window staring out over the city of Phoenix. After hanging up on the women and hearing Alinna's words, Dante couldn't even understand what was going on inside his head. At the moment, he just wasn't sure where his emotions were.

Raising his cell phone that was given to him, Dante looked at the screen. He found the number that Carlos told him was the direct contact line to Dominic. He hit "send" to call the number.

"Saldana" Dominic answered after three rings.

"Alright!"

Quiet for a moment, Dominic finally asked, "Am I to take your statement as you accepting my offer, Dante?"

"Yeah! I'm accepting it. But there's a few things we need to discuss and understand if I'ma be working for you."

"Very well, Dante," Dominic replied. "I would like for you to be here at my home by 10 o'clock and on time. We can talk while we ride to the meeting I have tomorrow."

Dante wrote down the address he was given and then hung up with Dominic. He then called Tony T and Dre, telling both of his boys to come to his room so he could discuss the new plans with them.

Within five minutes, while still standing at the window, he heard a knock on the door. Dante turned from the window and went to answer the door.

"What's up, bruh?" Tony T asked after Dante opened the door as he and Dre walked into his hotel room.

"We got a change of plans, fellas," Dante told them as he picked up his box of Black & Mild's from the dresser next to his Glock.

Seeing the look on Dante's face, Dre asked, "Fam, this shit got something to do with you talking with this Dominican dude?"

Nodding his head, Dante lifted his eyes up from lighting the Black and looked toward Dre, meeting his boy's eyes. He pulled on the Black until the tip was fully lit. While blowing thick cigar smoke, he said, "I want you two to head back to Miami."

"What?"

"Fuck is you talking about?"

Tony T and Dre responded at the same time, with Dre adding, "Dante, what's up? We not hitting this nigga Victor no more?"

"Check it, fellas!" Dante told them. He went on explaining the offer from Dominic and his decision to accept it. However, he wanted them both to head back home and look after the family until he was finished in Arizona.

"You joking, right?" Dre asked, staring hard at Dante. "What type of shit is you on, nigga? I ain't going nowhere without you, fam!"

"I wasn't asking!" Dante replied, staring straight back at Dre. "This my decision, and we not about to discuss it."

"Bruh, come on!" Tony T spoke up. "You asking us to just leave you up here with no back up, and you don't know shit about these muthafuckers. Yeah! You do ya thing when it comes to putting in work, but even you can be bodied."

"If that day comes, then it'll be a whole lot of muthafuckers walking that dark road with me," Dante replied, but then said, "I'm

43

meeting up with Dominic tomorrow and letting him know both of y'all handling getting the work back to Miami."

"You dead serious, ain't you?" Dre asked, heated as he stood staring at Dante.

Shifting his eyes from staring at Tony T and looking into Dre's angry eyes, Dante added, "When have I ever played about business, family? This what it is. Period!"

* * *

"Vanessa!"

Rolling over onto her back and looking up to her bedroom door as Alinna burst inside yelling her name, Vanessa looked down at her nephew to see D.J. was still asleep. She looked back at Alinna while holding her cell phone up to her ear and asked, "What do you want, Alinna?"

"Bitch, don't play with me!" Alinna yelled, only to get Vanessa to respond angrily. "Alinna, I promise you, if you wake up my nephew, we are going to have a real problem."

"We already have a real problem!" Alinna told her, staring hard at Vanessa. "How the fuck you gonna set me up like that? Why the fuck would you call me with Dante on the phone and not warn me he was on the phone?"

"Hold on!" Vanessa told her, rolling her eyes as she focused back on the phone. "Andre, baby, let me call you back. Tell Dante I got his message and call me later tomorrow after he handles his business."

Hanging up the phone with Dre, Vanessa focused back on Alinna but she never got the chance to say anything. Alinna beat her to the point saying, "What the hell you mean, Dante's message? And what business is he handling, Vanessa?"

"If you would have been paying attention and not all up in some new nigga face, you would know what's going on."

"Vanessa, don't fucking play with me. What's going on with Dante?"

Shaking her head as she sat staring at Alinna, Vanessa climbed out of bed and headed for the door, dragging Alinna out into the hallway and shutting the door behind them.

Facing Alinna, Vanessa angrily said, "Dante set it for both Dre and Tony T to bring back 50 bricks and 50 pounds. Dre says that that's just until Dante gets right up there in Arizona."

"So he's really not coming back then?"

"Isn't that what the fuck you wanted?"

"Vanessa, don't play with me!" Alinna screamed. "You know I don't really want Dante up there. He needs to be here with his family."

"Family, huh?" Vanessa repeated, staring at Alinna like she was crazy. "I'm surprised you remembered you had a family with Dante. That man has done everything he knew how and even now when you showing him your ass, he's still doing more all because he gives a fuck about you and the rest of us, even if you don't care about him. I'm happy he's staying where he is. Truthfully, Alinna, I hope he finds someone that realizes what type of dude he is because Dante is really one of a kind and you too stupid to realize what he was."

Unable to believe how Vanessa just talked to her and the shit she just told her, Alinna stood in the hallway staring at Vanessa's closed bedroom door into which her supposed best friend just walked.

Sucking her teeth, Alinna turned and marched to her own bedroom.

6

Waiting outside the hotel parking lot, Dante leaned against the front passenger door of the rented Explorer and smoked one of his Blacks from a new pack he bought earlier. Dante stood waiting for both Dre and Tony T to pick him up and drop him off out at Dominic's spot.

Dante checked his Mickey Mouse watch. It was already 9 o'clock. He had woken up at 8:00 a.m. to make sure to have enough time to find Dominic's crib. He looked up towards the front entrance of the hotel and saw his boys exiting the hotel, carrying their bags. He also noticed the expression on their faces.

Once Dre unlocked the SUV doors, Dante climbed up front while Tony T climbed in the back seat. Dre angrily climbed behind the wheel, tossing his bags to the back.

"Everything already ready and waiting for y'all when we get to Dominic's spot," Dante explained to both Dre and Tony T while Dre was pulling out of the parking spot.

Receiving no response from either of his boys, Dante read the address to Dre. There was still no response. He understood what was up with the both of them.

There was complete silence the entire 20-minute drive inside the Explorer. Dre finally pulled the truck up in front of a tall, black-painted security gate with an armed guard posted at the front. Dante leaned over towards Dre as the driver's window slid down and said, "I'm here for Mr. Saldana."

"And you are, sir?" the guard asked, while looking around inside the truck.

"Dante Blackwell," he replied, shifting his eyes to the side mirror and seeing a Mercedes limo pulling up behind the Explorer.

"Mr. Saldana is expecting you, Mr. Blackwell," the guard told Dante, stepping over to the security booth.

"Go ahead, fam!" Dante told Dre, as the gate slowly swung inward.

Dante watched as Dre drove up the wrap-around driveway, pulling up in front of a huge-as hell house that looked like something straight out of a movie. Dante waited until Dre had parked the Explorer near the front door. As he climbed out, the same limo at the front gate pulled up behind the SUV.

Dante stared back at the limo and watched as a huge, muscular Spanish man climbed out of the back seat and stared straight in his direction. He turned his attention to the front door of the mansion to see a team of suit-wearing security fall out of the house. Dominic stepped outside behind them and smiled at Dante.

"Dante!" Dominic said as he walked out to greet him.

"Mr. Saldana," Dante replied, shaking the Dominican drug lord's hand.

"Daddy!"

Both Dominic and Dante turned around and looked back at the limo.

"Natalie!" Dominic happily said. He spit out a few words in rapid Spanish as his daughter walked up and into his open arms.

While looking at both her father and Dante staring at her, Natalie asked her father who the man was in front of her.

Surprising both Dominic and his daughter, Dante spoke in perfect Spanish, "Allow me to introduce myself. I'm your dad's new bodyguard, Dante Blackwell."

47

Smiling as she stared at Mr. Blackwell, Natalie turned back to her father and, in Spanish, asked, "Why didn't you tell me that you decided to take on a new bodyguard?"

Dominic shifted his eyes to his left to see his Bentley pulling around to the front. He focused back on his daughter and, in English, replied, "We will talk later. Mr. Blackwell and I have business to discuss before my meeting this afternoon. Your mother is inside waiting."

Nodding her head in acceptance, Natalie kissed her father's cheek and then turned slowly back to Dante. In English, but with a Spanish accent, she said, "It was good to have met you, Mr. Blackwell. Hopefully we will have the chance to meet again so that you and I may talk."

"Hopefully," Dante replied, watching Natalie as she walked away, trailed by the big Spanish dude.

"That is Gomez," Dominic spoke up, watching Dante as he stood watching both Natalie and his daughter's personal bodyguard.

"Bodyguard?" Dante asked, looking toward Dominic who slowly nodded yes.

"Have your friends drive around back. Everything is ready for them. Then you can join me inside my car. We need to get going."

As the Dominican drug lord walked off, heading toward his Bentley where his head of security, Carlos, stood waiting with the back door opened, Dante turned back to the Ford Explorer. He stepped in front of the passenger window, and leaning inside said, "Everything already set up and ready. Drive 'round back and pick it up, fellas."

"So, that's it, nigga?" Tony T asked, as he sat forward to stare at Dante.

"You niggas just make sure y'all hit me up when y'all touch down in the M.I.A., alright?" Dante told both his boys.

Then he went to turn and walk off and stopped only to hear, "Don't try to have all the fun yourself, fam. Hit us up if you need us."

Looking back inside the Explorer passenger window over to his best friend, who was like his brother, Dante said simply, "Just make sure when I do call, shit good at the house and you niggas ready. Love!"

Hearing both his boys responses at his showing of affection, Dante tapped the side of the Explorer as he walked off and headed over towards the Bentley.

Dante nodded to Carlos, who opened the back car door for him and returned the nod. Dante returned his cell phone to him, thanked him, and then climbed into the back seat of the Bentley, where Dominic was on the phone speaking Spanish.

Trying to ignore the conversation that Dominic was having, yet catching enough of it to know it was about Victor Fayman, Dante felt the Bentley begin moving. He turned his attention outside the window as the car drove away from the mansion.

"So, Dante," Dominic started as he hung up his cell phone, "what is it that you mentioned that we needed to discuss?"

Dante turned his head and met the Dominican's dark brown eyes. He explained to his new employer, "You're paying me to do the whole bodyguard thing. Cool! I'ma take care of that. But you need to understand that I don't know how you may have your boys handling business. If I pull my heat, I'm more than likely gonna use them, and I don't need you questioning what I do. I'm a respect you as my employer, but you need to respect me as the muthafucker that's gonna keep you alive. Do we agree on that?"

Showing a small smile as he nodded his head in agreement, Dominic then asked, "Are you carrying now?"

"Always!" Dante answered, patting the space at the front of his pants where one of his bangers was.

Leaning forward, Dominic reached and picked up a black plastic bag that sat on the floor at his left foot and handed it to Dante saying, "These are yours now. We will be getting rid of the weapons you're carrying now."

Taking the bag from his employer, Dante asked the Dominican what the problem was with what he was carrying.

"Let's just say that your new weapons are better suited for you," Dominic replied, as he answered his ringing phone.

Focusing on what he was given, Dante opened the plastic bag and looked inside. He reached in and pulled out what he easily recognized as a shoulder holster.

It was a double holster with two burners already inside. Dante set the plastic bag back down, still feeling weight inside, as he focused on the two bangers inside the shoulder holster.

Grabbing one of the burners, Dante smiled at the chrome and pearl-handled .45 automatic.

"I take it from your expression that you approve of the choice of weapons I've picked out for you," Dominic inquired, watching Dante as he checked the new .45s.

Slamming the magazine back inside the banger and then cocking it, Dante smirked as he cut his eyes back over to Dominic and stated, "Yeah! These will definitely work."

* * *

Leaving her trap spot after dropping off re-up work to her crew and picking up the money they had, Vanessa was headed across town to Liberty City to drop off more work. Her mind was on both Dante and Dre. She was expecting to hear from them this morning and, honestly, she was a little worried.

Once she got to Liberty City, Vanessa made her drop-offs and picked up more money. She heard her crew was having a little trouble with some niggas who were working for some clown named Ghost. Vanessa told her crew to let her know if she needed to handle the problem if it continued and they couldn't take care of things.

Leaving the Liberty City spot, Vanessa pulled out her ringing cell phone and glanced down to see Harmony calling. "What's up, girl? Where you at?"

"I'm at the spot," Harmony answered and then asked, "Nessa, what's up? You talk to Alinna?"

"No, girl! Her ass was gone when I woke up. Why? What's up?"

"I just been trying to call her about some business that was brought to me. I wanna see what she think."

"Harmony, I don't know what the hell...hold on a second," Vanessa switched up, hearing her line beep.

Looking at the screen, she smiled and saw that it was Dre calling her. Vanessa told Harmony she'd call her right back and then she switched over to Dre. "Hey, baby! What's up?"

"What up, Nessa? You busy?"

"Not right now. Why? What's up? Everything okay?"

"Yeah! Everything good," Dre answered. "We on our back track to Miami, though."

"So Dante still staying in Arizona?"

"Yeah, but we got what he promised."

'You sound upset."

"I just hate leaving my nigga there without me. Who gonna watch his back?"

"Andre, you know as well as I do that Dante can take care of his self. I've never met someone that does the shit he does. I'm sure if he needs you or Tony T, he'll call y'all."

"That's what the fuck his crazy ass said before we left," Dre told Vanessa. "I been thinking also. How you feel about us getting our own shit?"

"You mean moving out the house?"

"Yeah!"

"Why?" Vanessa asked. "What about the others, Andre?"

"I'ma be real with you, Nessa," Dre told his woman. "I really want outta that house because of ya girl Alinna. She the reason my nigga where he at now because of her bullshit."

Sighing deeply and blowing into the receiver, Vanessa was really unable to go against what her man was saying so she simply said, "Baby, look! Can we talk about this when you get back home, please?"

"Yeah, whatever!" Dre replied. "We should be there by Tuesday night."

"I love you!"

"Yeah! I love you, too, Nessa!"

Hearing the way Dre sounded before he hung up, Vanessa gave another deep sigh just as she heard her cell phone go off again. Looking down, she saw it was her girl Amber calling.

* * *

Walking alongside Dominic as the two of them exited out of the building after his new employer finished his meeting with the five other supposed businessmen, Dante allowed the security team to cover them as they approached the Bentley.

Getting a nod from Carlos, Dante climbed into the Bentley behind his employer. Carlos shut the car door behind both of them.

"So tell me, Dante," Dominic said as the Bentley pulled off, "what did you think of the meeting?"

Looking over to his employer, Dante met Dominic's stare and after a moment said, "I think everybody at that meeting was full of shit and the dude Stevens is a problem that needs to be handled before he becomes an even bigger problem."

"I agree fully!" Dominic replied, adding more to the conversation to see how Dante would respond. "But the problem with dealing with Stevens is that he is the biggest heroin dealer in Phoenix. He's connected with some very powerful Japanese people who I've been trying to get into business with. Because of Stevens dealings with the Japanese, I've been unable to connect with the business that they would be willing to start with me."

Looking back over at Dominic, Dante met his employer's stare to let him know he caught on to what his employer was hinting at. He then turned and looked back out the car window, saying after a moment, "Get me the information on Stevens, and I'll handle the rest."

Dominic slowly smiled, realizing his new employee caught on to what he was hinting at. He pulled out his cell phone.

Dante allowed his mind to drift back to Alinna and Angela, along with both his son and daughter, forcing him to lose his train of thought until Dominic called out to him. He turned his attention back to his employer and replied, "Yeah, what's up?"

"How taller are you, Dante?" Dominic asked, as he stared over at Dante with his cell phone in his ear.

"5' 11."

"Your weight?"

"197 pounds."

Nodding his head, Dominic turned his attention back to his phone call to pass on the information he had just received. He explained that they would be back to the mansion in a little while.

Hanging up the phone, Dominic turned back to Dante and asked, "Do you drive, Dante?"

"You mean, do I chauffeur?"

"No, my friend," Dominic answered, laughing at seeing Dante's facial expression. "I mean, can you drive or would you rather be chauffeured?"

"I plan to take care of finding some wheels whenever I catch some free time. I also gotta find a spot to live close by."

Nodding his head in response to Dante, Dominic grinned as he dug out a cigar from the inner pocket of his suit jacket.

* * *

They made it back to the mansion and waited until the Bentley came to a full stop out front. Dante opened the car door just as the driver was rushing around to open it for him and Dominic.

Dante nodded at the driver, who smirked and nodded back at him. Dante then stood to the side as Dominic stepped out of the Bentley as Carlos walked up.

"You're free until tonight, Carlos," Dominic told his head of security. "Remember, we're leaving for the business dinner with Malcolm Pierce."

"Yes, sir, Mr. Saldana," Carlos replied, as both Dante and Dominic walked off and headed towards the front door of the mansion.

Leading Dante to the front door of his estate, where one of seven staff members was holding open the door, Dominic said to Dante over his shoulder, "Come. I'll introduce you to the staff as well as the mistress of the mansion."

Following Dominic inside, Dante stood beside his employer as six other staff members showed up, listening as members introduced themselves to him.

"So, this is the young man I've been hearing non-stop about?"

Dante looked over to the far right and saw a slim but nicely built older version of Dominic's daughter, Natalie, ask the question. Dante looked to Dominic who happily said, "Carmen, my wife! Come and meet Mr. Dante Blackwell."

"I feel like I already know him," Carmen stated with a smile, as she walked over to Dante with her hand held out.

"It's good to meet you, Mrs. Saldana!" Dante said, smiling at the older woman while being a bit surprised at how gorgeous she looked.

"I see that my daughter was correct when describing you," Carmen replied looking Dante over with a grin. "You really are extremely handsome, Mr. Blackwell."

"Thank you, Mrs. Saldana!" Dante answered before adding, "Please, call me Dante."

"As long as you call me Carmen," she told Dante while still smiling. She looked over at her husband as he stood smiling and watching her with Dante. "My love, you've had a few calls. I've left messages in your office. Why don't you go and check them while I show Dante around his new residence."

"Very well!" Dominic replied with a smile as he kissed his wife. He turned to Dante and said, "We leave for dinner at 10:00 tonight. I will see you then."

Nodding his head in response, Dante looked back at Carmen as she announced, "Come Dante! Let me show you around the place."

Allowing Carmen to wrap her arm around his left arm and leading him further into the mansion, Dante found himself walking alongside the older woman and touring the two-story, 7-bedroom, 3-bathroom home, complete with an elevator. It even had a chef-style kitchen that looked like it belonged in a restaurant, which included three chefs who worked on staff.

Carmen then led him outside behind the mansion to a detached guesthouse that was a two-minute walk away from the home's back entrance. Dante laughed as Carmen led him into the guesthouse. It looked like a smaller version of the mansion itself with two bedrooms, two baths and its own pool and spa outside.

"What do you think, Dante?" Carmen asked, smiling at him as he stood beside her and looked around.

"What do I think, huh?" Dante repeated. "This is some place you guys live in. I'm really impressed!"

"I'm happy you approve," Carmen told him. "This will be where you will be living. I figured you would want your own place and space."

Nodding his head in approval, Dante thanked the older woman as he continued looking around the guesthouse.

"I'll leave you to look around, Dante," Carmen told him, handing him a set of keys. "When you're finished looking around, come back to the house. There's something else Dominic and I have for you."

Dante watched as Carmen walked out of the guesthouse door. Then he turned back around to look at his new home. He first walked to the nice-sized kitchen that was done up in white and marble.

Then he made his way from the kitchen through the living room, which led to two bedrooms. He walked into the master bedroom's bath, which had a standing-glass, sliding shower door and a Jacuzzi-style bathtub. Dante shook his head, smirking as he turned and walked back out into the master bedroom.

He stopped in front of the walk-in closet and saw all the different styles of suits and urban clothes. Dante lowered his eyes to the racks filled with different styles of dress shoes and even…

Dante immediately snatched his banger from the left-side holster that Dominic had given him. He shifted his body and turned towards the bedroom door. Dante was seconds away from pulling the trigger when he recognized who walked into the room.

"Whoa! It's just me!" Natalie cried, throwing up both her hands and falling back against the bedroom door, staring wide-eyed at Dante.

"You should announce yourself when you walk into a room," Dante told her as he lowered his gun.

"How did you know I was there?" she asked as she lowered her hands and relaxed.

"I heard the front door when it opened," Dante answered. "What are you doing here?'

"You don't sound happy to see me, Dante?" Natalie asked him, with a fake pouting look on her face.

Shaking his head as he slid his hammer back into his holster, he turned back to the closet and asked, "What do you want, Natalie?"

"Actually, I wanted to see you. I'm also supposed to show you what's outside for you."

"What are you talking about?"

With a big smile, Natalie walked over to Dante and took his hand, leading him from the closet toward the bedroom door and said, "Just come with me. You'll like what I've got to show you."

7

Dante allowed Dominic's daughter to drag him back through the mansion, passing a smiling Carmen, who was walking out of one of the many rooms on the first floor. Dante found himself being pulled out the front door and then down the walkway around to the far side of the mansion where a metallic-gray Benz was parked in front of a five-car garage.

"What do you think?" Natalie asked, turning and smiling back at Dante.

"What?" Dante asked confused, looking straight at Natalie.

"The car, Dante!" Natalie answered with a giggle. She turned Dante around to the driver's side of the Mercedes. "This is your new car, Dante."

"What?" Dante exclaimed in both disbelief and confusion.

"What my daughter is telling you, Dante," Carmen began, as she and two security guards walked over from the front of the house, "is that this is a gift from both Dominic and me."

"I picked it out," Natalie told him, still smiling at Dante.

Looking back to Carmen from Natalie, Dante met the older woman's eyes and said, "What's this all about? I could have bought my own ride."

"We're well aware of that, Mr. Blackwell," Carmen replied smiling at him. "My husband did a background check on you and we are fully aware of what you are able to do. This is our way of saying that we want you to feel welcome and at home here with us."

"Dante, come on! Let's go for a ride!" Natalie screamed, rushing around to the passenger side of the Benz.

"The key is already attached to the ring I handed to you earlier, Dante," Carmen told him, as she turned and walked away. She turned back around and said, "Enjoy yourself!"

"Dante! Come on!" Natalie cried out, waving to get Dante's attention.

Dante looked at Carmen as she was walking away and then focused back on Natalie. He looked down at the Mercedes Benz S-class coupe that was just given to him. Then he dug out the keys from inside his pocket and hit the remote that was also a key. Both he and Natalie climbed inside onto creamy, brown-leather seats.

He checked out the new smart phone-style console, touch-pad perches over a command-system control knob that operated numerous vehicle functions. Dante looked around the car, nodding in approval at what he was seeing.

"Are you just going to sit there or are we going for a ride, Dante?" Natalie spoke up, smiling over at him.

Shifting his eyes over to Natalie, Dante shook his head. He smiled as he pushed the button that started the Mercedes engine. He glanced back over at Natalie as he reversed the Benz from in front of the garage.

* * *

Carmen watched from the front door as both Dante and her daughter drove away inside the new Mercedes. She smiled and stepped back inside the house, closing and locking the door behind her. She turned and started towards the side hallway leading to her husband's office.

She lightly knocked and pushed open the thick, oil-shined redwood office door. Stepping inside her husband's office, she saw Dominic seated behind his desk speaking on the phone. Carmen met her husband's eyes as he held up his hand for her to hold on.

Taking a seat in one of the two cushioned chairs in front of her husband's desk, Carmen crossed her long and slim, nicely muscular, legs. She smiled at her husband. His eyes shifted from the papers on top of his desk in front of him to her legs and then up to her eyes.

"I will call you back," Dominic said into the phone, holding his wife's eyes as he hung up the phone. He smiled at Carmen and said, "What is it, my love?"

"I wanted to inform you that I was able to get Mr. Blackwell to accept our gift, "Carmen told her husband, before adding, "It may also have had a little to do with your daughter as well, my husband."

Making a face, Dominic asked, "Exactly what does Natalie have to do with Dante?"

"It seems that our daughter may have taken an interest in Mr. Dante Blackwell," Carmen told her husband, with a small smile.

"Where is she?"

"Both Dante and Natalie have left. He's taken her for a ride at our daughter's request."

Leaning back in his cushion, black-leather office desk chair, Dominic folded his hands around his chest and said, "Where is Gomez?"

"My guess would be that he's inside his room as was told of him," Carmen answered. "I'm pretty sure that Gomez will be upset once he hears Natalie has left without him."

Slowly smiling as he stared across at his wife, Dominic said, "You questioned me about Dante's ability and sureness with wanting to hire him. This is the perfect timing for a display."

"What are you planning, Dominic?" Carmen asked her husband, staring at him with a funny expression on her face.

Smiling a little more, Dominic answered, "Just wait and see, my wife. Wait and see!"

* * *

Pulling in front of Alex's condo, Alinna saw his Cadillac parked outside. She parked her BMW beside his car and shut off the engine.

Alinna grabbed her bag and climbed out of her car. As she was locking it up, she heard a voice from her left side: "What's up, beautiful?"

She smiled seeing Alex standing in the doorway to his condominium dressed in gray cotton sweatpants and a white wife beater. She silently cursed herself as she found herself comparing Alex to Dante.

She was still smiling as she walked from the car and headed toward his front door. Alinna went up on her toes and kissed Alex on the lips and said, "Hey, sexy! You look like you missed me!"

"More than you know!" Alex replied, smiling as he took Alinna's hand and pulled her gently inside the condo. He closed and locked the door behind them.

Alinna was impressed when she looked around the condo. She heard Alex tell her to make herself at home, as he headed towards the kitchen. She slowly made her way through to the den, checking out the hook-up.

Alinna nodded her head at the setup Alex had in his den. She stopped in front of the picture display, as she found herself looking for females in pictures with Alex. She noticed an exotic-looking female who showed up in more than one photo with Alex, even though she looked much younger than Alex did.

"That's my baby sister you're staring at!" Alex spoke up, as he walked up behind her.

Looking from the photos back over her shoulder at Alex's face, Alinna waited until he looked down meeting her eyes and said, "You sure that's your sister, Alex?"

"Would I lie?"

"I don't know," she answered. A moment later she asked, "Would you lie to me, Alex?"

"Come on!" he told Alinna, taking her hand and leading her over to the sofa. They sat down and he pulled her beside him. "Alinna, listen! I'm not a fool, beautiful. I can see the hurt in your eyes and I know it was a guy before me that put that hurt there. But I'm not him. I don't want to be him but I do want you, though. I understand we've only known each other a short time but I know that it's you I want. I want this friendship to become a serious relationship. I want us to build something you can believe in but only if it's also what you want."

Shaking her head and sighing loudly, Alinna broke eye contract with Alex and said, "Alex, there's a lot you don't know about me. First, you should know that although I do like you a lot, I'm still in love with my son's father, even though we're no longer together."

"Where is he now?"

"He left town."

"Is he coming back?"

"I'm not really sure," Alinna answered truthfully, before adding, "I don't think he will though."

"So, basically, what you're telling me is that our chances of having anything aren't great because you're still in love with your son's father, even though he hurt you?"

Looking back and meeting Alex's eyes, Alinna said, "I want you, Alex. I won't lie to you. But my trust isn't really great right now. I can only promise you that I will give things between us a real try if you're willing to give me time."

Alex reached up and gently brushed back Alinna's hair and lightly ran the back of his hand down the side of her face. Alex smiled as he replied, "Whatever it takes to make you mine, Alinna. I'm willing to endure whatever. I want you that badly."

Smiling a bit as Alex leaned towards her, Alinna reached up and wrapped her arms around his neck, while accepting the kiss he laid on her lips.

* * *

Dante drove the smooth-riding Benz up the drive back to the mansion and saw the crowd of security already posted out front. He also noticed both Carmen and Dominic standing outside the mansion doorway. Dante heard Natalie mumble something about Gomez, which directed his attention to the big man posted in front of the house just a bit further down from where her parents stood on the porch.

Pulling the Benz to a stop in front of the crowd of security team, Dante parked the car as a chauffeur rushed over around to the driver's door. He noticed the big Spanish man snatch open the passenger-side door and grab Natalie aggressively out of the seat.

"Gomez!" Natalie cried, pulling and trying to get away from her bodyguard's grip. "What is wrong with you? Let me go this minute!"

"You are not supposed to leave without me!" Gomez said, as he pressed his face angrily up into Natalie's face.

"You are out of line. Release me now!" Natalie yelled, still trying to get away from her bodyguard.

"You will never leave without . . ."

"You may wanna let her go," Dante stated, as he calmly walked up beside both Natalie and the bodyguard.

"You will be dealt with shortly," Gomez told the new guy, pushing Dante away. He then turned his attention back to Natalie.

Dante caught Gomez's hand by the top of his fingers and bent them backwards, causing the guy to cry out in pain. Dante then slammed his elbow into Gomez's nose, snapping his head back. At the same time, he kicked his left leg out from under him and sent homeboy backwards to the pavement.

He then grabbed his banger from his right holster with his left hand, while still holding Gomez's fingers in his right hand. Dante had the .45 pressed to the front of Gomez's forehead by the time he opened his eyes and was looking up at Dante.

"Enough!" Dominic yelled out, drawing everyone's attention to him including Dante who cut his eyes up to his new employer before focusing back on Gomez. "Release him, Dante! He's okay now."

Doing as he was told and releasing the muscular bodyguard's hand while keeping his hammer out gripped it in his left hand, Dante grabbed Natalie and pulled her behind him. He watched

Gomez slowly climb to one knee and wipe the blood away from his busted and bleeding nose.

"Do you still question my decision, my wife?" Dominic asked Carmen, while showing a small smile toward Dante, who was escorting Natalie toward the front door.

"He is better than I expected, my husband," Carmen replied with a grin. "He is really fast also. Did you see how fast he took down Gomez and had his firearm out and pointed at Gomez?"

"I'm glad you approve, my wife," Dominic said, just as Natalie rushed passed to her mother while Dante stopped in front of him.

"What's up with homeboy?" Dante asked, nodding back over his shoulder down to where Gomez was being helped up by a few members of the security team.

"Pay Gomez no attention, Dante," Dominic said, with a wave of the hand. "He is very overprotective when it comes to my daughter. Come with me."

Looking over to Natalie before following behind Dominic, Dante met her eyes and asked, "You alright?"

Nodding her head yes, she stood watching as Dante followed behind her father. She then heard her mother say, "While you were out with Dante Jonathan called to speak to you."

"Who?" Natalie asked, still staring after Dante.

Slowly smiling, Carmen wrapped her arms around her daughter and led her back into the house saying, "You do remember Jonathan Hernandez, the friend you've been seeing, right?"

* * *

Following Dominic into his office where Carlos was waiting, Dante nodded to him and took a seat on the sofa across the room. Dominic walked around behind his desk and sat down.

"Okay, gentlemen," Dominic began, as he leaned forward and rested his arms atop the desk. He folded his hands together as he looked from Carlos to Dante. "This meeting tonight is very important and the gentleman I'm meeting with is coming all the way from Los Angles. The problem is that the meeting is at a restaurant located in Victor Fayman's part of town and this meeting really isn't a secret, so I'm expecting..."

"...him to show up and cause a little scene, right?" Dante finished his sentence, as he sat unwrapping one of the Black & Mild's he pulled from the fresh box he bought on the way back to the mansion with Natalie.

Dominic allowed a small smile to show on his lips as he sat staring at Dante and said, "After what happened on Victor's birthday the other night, I'm pretty sure that he is planning to react for what happened to him in front of the whole nightclub."

"Why not relocate to a different spot to have this meeting at?" Dante asked, as he motioned for permission to light up and smoke.

Waving an okay for Dante to smoke, Dominic followed, "The problem with relocating for this meeting, Dante, is that this is the location Mr. and Mrs. Russell have decided on. It is near the hotel where they will be staying and it's a favorite restaurant of Mrs. Russell."

"So, let me get this right," Dante spoke up again, blowing thick cigar smoke up into the air. "Not only is this meeting in this dude Victor's area but this business friend is also bringing his wife as well?"

"Exactly!" Dominic answered.

"So, I'm guessing also that Mrs. Saldana is coming with you?" Dante asked, while shaking his head before Dominic could actually answer, seeing the bullshit before it actually went down.

Dominic discussed a few more things concerning the up-and-coming meeting as well as other business issues. He wanted to bring Dante up to date for security reasons. Dante sat listening to both his new employer and the head of security, asking a few questions of his own while throwing out a few suggestions on what he thought about the plans. Even Dominic thought a few of Dante's ideas sounded good and said he would consider them.

Once the meeting was over and Dominic dismissed him and Carlos to take a phone call, Dante followed Carlos outside the office and grabbed his arm as he was pulling the office door shut.

"Whoa!" Dante said, as he stopped the head of security. "We need to talk, playboy."

"What is the problem, Mr. Blackwell, sir?" Carlos asked, turning toward Dante.

"We gotta few hours before we leaving for this hook-up with this business friend of Dominic's. I want us to take a trip out to this restaurant and check the spot out before heading out there."

Nodding his head in agreement, Carlos expressed that he wanted to let a few of his men know he was leaving and would meet Dante out front.

Turning and walking off toward the front of the mansion, Dante was just reaching for the door handle when he heard, "Dante, wait!"

Looking back over his shoulder, he saw Natalie rushing down the stairs. He turned to face her as she slowly walked up to him with a smile.

"What's up, Natalie?"

"Where are you going?" she asked, still smiling at Dante.

"Me and Carlos about to make a quick run and handle something," Dante explained. "What's up, though? You all right?"

Nodding her head yes, she continued, "Dante, I was wondering if you would like to go with me to this fundraising event that's happening this weekend. A friend of mine is having it."

"It sounds cool but let me get with your dad and see what he got planned for this weekend, alright?"

Smiling as she laid her hand into Dante's chest, Natalie thanked him and rushed off.

Watching Natalie as she rushed off towards the far left-side hallway, Dante shook his head and smiled. As he turned to leave, he stopped and looked at the top of the stairwell to find Carmen Saldana standing there with a smile as she watched him. Then she turned around and walked off, down the upstairs hallway and out of sight.

8

Dante stood outside the mansion talking with Carlos when bo-th Dominic and Carmen stepped out of the front door. Dante watched from the corner of his eye as the security team surrounded the couple. He quickly noticed the expression on Carmen's face as she headed down the steps to the Mercedes limo, which he and Carlos were standing next to.

Stepping away from the limo and approaching Dominic and Carmen, Dante dismissed the security team and fell in step behind them, receiving a smile from Carmen before she turned her focus back to her husband.

Once the Saldanas were inside the back of the limo, Dante nodded to Carlos as he climbed inside, closing the limo door behind him.

"Dante, you look extremely handsome in that suit," Carmen told him, smiling, as she looked Dante over in the Armani suit he was wearing.

"Thanks!" Dante replied, smiling back at Carmen. "You look gorgeous yourself."

"Too bad Natalie didn't get the chance to see you before she left. She picked that suit out herself," Carmen told him, smiling even more as she stared straight into Dante's beautiful eyes.

"Where did you and Carlos leave to after our meeting earlier, Dante?" Dominic asked, as he read the text from his cell phone.

"I wanted to get a look at the area this restaurant was in and check out a few things just in case," Dante explained, just as the cell phone he was given vibrated inside his suit pants pocket.

Pulling out the new touch-screen, Dante saw that Vanessa was calling him. He immediately sent it to voicemail. He shot a quick text message to her explaining that he couldn't talk, but he would call her back when he was free.

"So Dante," Carmen said, getting Dante's attention. "Where exactly did you learn to fight? That was an impressive display that I saw earlier. You must know some type of fighting to take someone as big as Gomez down so easily."

"Truthfully, a friend of my father's was in the Marines," Dante told Carmen. He further explained, "He taught me the only style he knew."

"Guerilla warfare!" Dominic spoke up, drawing both Dante and his wife's attention over to him.

Nodding his head and seeing the smile on Dominic's face, Dante said, "That's pretty much right! He taught me exactly what the service taught him."

"So, where are your father and this friend now, Dante?" Carmen asked.

"My father's dead," Dante answered. "He died when I turned 16. But my father's friend lives in North Dakota now with his wife and daughter."

"What about your mother?" Carmen asked.

"I never met her," Dante answered.

"So, do you have any family, Dante?" Dominic asked, drawing Dante's attention to him.

Quiet a moment as he shifted his eyes over and outside the limo window, Dante looked back to his employer and answered, "I have a daughter and a son but they both live with their mothers."

"Are you with either of your children's mothers, Dante?" Carmen asked.

Shaking his head no, Dante continued, "I was with my son's mother but she's with someone else. As far as my daughter's mother, that's a whole different story. Let's just say that her choice of employment keeps us from being together."

"She works for the law, doesn't she?" Dominic asked him.

"She's a captain for the M.D.P.D."

"You'll have to tell me how you ending up with a captain of the Miami Department," Carmen said, smiling as she stared at Dante with a new interest in her eyes.

* * *

Dante was the first one out of the limo once the driver pulled up in front of the five-star restaurant's front entrance. Dante glanced around sharply as both Dominic and Carmen climbed from the limo behind him.

Dante checked and saw that both ends of the street were blocked off by Dominic's security team, along with a number of them at the parking lot entrance, keeping away other guests. Dante waved off the valet as he followed close behind the Saldanas, as they entered the restaurant.

He looked back outside the glass entrance door and met Carlos's stare. Dante nodded and turned back to face the Saldanas. He heard the hostess tell Dominic and Carmen that their table and guests were waiting for them.

Taking her husband and wrapping her arm through his, Carmen followed alongside him, as they made their way to the table. She glanced back to look at Dante to find him gone.

"Dominic! Dante's not…"

"Aaron Russell!" Dominic said, as he and Carmen stopped at the table where they were meeting with Mr. Russell and his wife.

"Dominic Saldana!" Aaron said, as he stood from his seat to shake Dominic's hand. He looked at his wife and said, "Carmen, how are you?"

"I'm wonderful, Aaron!" Carmen replied with a smile.

"Carmen, it's good to see you again," Dianna said, as she stepped around her husband to hug Carmen.

"Dianna, it's wonderful to see you as well," Carmen replied, as she released Mrs. Russell.

"Mrs. Saldana, your seat ma'am . . ."

"I have that!" Dante spoke up, as he appeared at Carmen's side catching the outstretched hand from the cocky suit-wearing host that was holding out the chair for her.

Carmen smiled at seeing Dante, wondering exactly where he had went and where he came from. She nodded her thanks to him and sat down in the seat he now held out for her, only to hear him whisper into her ear," If you want me, just say my name. I'm not far away."

She nodded her head as she adjusted in her seat with Dante's help. Carmen smiled her thanks and turned her attention back to the table.

Dominic nodded his approval after catching his eye for helping Carmen. He then turned his attention to Aaron, who asked, "Who's the new help, Dominic?"

"He's the new bodyguard, Aaron."

"He looks a little young to be a bodyguard."

"Maybe! But he's very good at what he does, Aaron. Believe me!"

"I'll take your word for it," Aaron replied, looking up as he found himself looking around for the young bodyguard. He was gone, however, as if he up and disappeared.

"Let's talk business, Aaron, so we can enjoy a night of dinner and catching up," Dominic said, switching into business mode.

* * *

"Natalie!" Jonathan Hernandez said.

Barely hearing her name, she looked up and across the table into her dinner date's hazel-brownish eyes. She forced a small smile asking Jonathan, "What did you say, Jonathan? I'm sorry. I didn't even hear you."

"Actually, I was asking you if you were alright," Jonathan told her. "You've been like you're somewhere else since we left your parents place."

"I guess I'm really not hungry, Jonathan," she told him. "Can we just leave, please?"

"Sure!" Jonathan replied, as he waved over the waiter.

Five minutes later the bill was paid, and they were standing out front of the restaurant when the valet pulled Jonathan's BMW around. Natalie climbed inside the passenger seat, while Jonathan walked around to the driver side.

Once he pulled out of the restaurant's parking lot and was driving away, Natalie sat staring out the passenger-side window.

Jonathan asked, "Natalie, what's the problem? What's going on with you?"

"Jonathan, it's nothing!"

"I'm sorry," Jonathan replied. "I can't accept that. I'm concerned about you."

"Don't be."

"It's a little hard not to."

Sighing deeply and loudly, Natalie turned to stare over at Jonathan and was just opening her mouth to explain what was wrong with her when Jonathan slammed on the brakes in the middle of the street.

"What the hell?" Jonathan yelled, as he stared at the black SUV that swung out in front of his car blocking his way.

Natalie stared at the SUV, watching the back door swing open as four armed men jumped out with semi-automatic rifles. She screamed at the first sound of a shot being fired and watched as one of the four gunmen slam backwards into the side of the SUV.

Unsure of what was going on as the streets were lit up with the sound of firing, Natalie screamed again when the passenger door was snatched open and she was grabbed.

"Jonathan, get down!" Gomez yelled over the shooting.

"Gomez!" Natalie cried. "What's going on?"

She didn't receive an answer and jumped when Gomez began shooting back at the gunmen over the passenger door through the now-blown out window

"Fuck!" Gomez yelled, seeing another SUV swing up with more gunmen jumping out.

Quickly climbing into the BMW, Gomez yelled for Jonathan to drive. The young boy, however, was too scared to get up off the floor.

"Fuck! Shit!" Gomez yelled out in Spanish.

* * *

"So, Aaron, do we have a new deal?" Dominic asked, as he held out his hand.

Smiling as he took Dominic's hand, Aaron shook hands and began, "We definitely have a…"

Dominic turned to his right as both Dante and Carlos walked up to the table. Noting their facial expressions, Dominic opened his mouth to ask if everything was all right. Dante bent down and whispered into his ear, "Something came up. I can't explain right now. Carlos knows what he's supposed to do and he'll explain."

"Dante, what's going on?" Carmen asked just as Dante took off in a run through the restaurant. She looked to her husband who was simply staring at Dante.

Dante burst out the front entrance door of the restaurant. He looked around and remembered he didn't drive that evening. He saw a pearl-white Porsche 911 Turbo that had pulled up as a blonde-haired woman climbed out the passenger side. Dante took off, rushed towards the valet, and intercepted the keys that the young white driver had just tossed through the air to the valet.

Ignoring the yell from the driver, Dante hopped inside the Porsche behind the wheel. He cranked up the car as the car owner grabbed his arm.

"What the fuck are . . . ?"

Punching him in the face and dropping him instantly, Dante slammed the car door shut and peeled out from the restaurant parking lot.

Digging out his cell phone, Dante punched in Natalie's number and listened to the line ring three times when Natalie answered loudly, "Hello?"

"Natalie! It's Dante. Put Go . . ."

"Oh my God, Dante! Where are you? We're being chased and shot at. Gomez is shot. We need help, Dante! Please, help us!"

"Natalie, relax!" Dante told her. "First, I need you to tell me where Gomez at."

"He's driving."

"Put 'em on the phone, Natalie."

Dante waited a few moments, hearing the engine to whatever car they were in, before he heard Gomez's Spanish accent say, "Yeah!"

"Gomez, this Dante! Where are you? I need to know where you are if I'm going to help."

* * *

Gomez hung up after telling Dante where he would meet him. He had given him directions to an empty shopping mall parking lot, after Dante requested he go to an open area. Gomez tossed the phone back to Natalie as she asked, "What's going on, Gomez? What did Dante say? Is my father sending help?"

"That's what Dante told me," Gomez answered, ignoring the questions she kept shooting at him.

Glancing into the rear-view mirror and seeing both SUVs right behind him, Gomez pressed down harder on the gas, feeling the BMW pick up speed as they pulled away a bit from the SUV pursuing them.

He arrived in the shopping center's parking lot where there were still a number of parked cars. Gomez kept driving and went past the lot, as he yelled back to Natalie to call Dante back.

"He's not answering!" she yelled. She then screamed upon hearing the loud blowout sound and seeing Gomez trying to handle the car that was now out of control.

"Hang on!" Gomez yelled, as he pulled the BMW into a hard right, swinging it down a side street beside a gas station, only to slam into a light pole causing the air bags to deploy.

Fighting to get out of the BMW, Natalie fell out of the car just as both SUVs swung down the street behind them. Natalie screamed as Gomez staggered around the front of the car up to her.

"Come on, Natalie!" Gomez said, grabbing her arm.

"Jonathan!" Natalie said, pulling away from Gomez and rushing back to the BMW.

"Natalie, we need to . . . "

Gomez ducked at hearing the canon-like sounds. He looked up for a second and stared in confusion before he realized he was watching Dante calmly and carelessly walking away from a pearl-white Porsche with both his guns in his hands. He was firing at the seven gunmen. He continued to watch as two guns and then another one dropped to the ground.

Gomez reloaded, jumped up, and yelled at Natalie to stay with the car. Gomez opened fire at the gunmen and saw the last four of them rushing to climb back into their SUV. One of them grabbed his side and fell down.

Watching the SUV speed off, Gomez rushed up to Dante as he stood over the one gunman holding his side and moaning in pain. He asked, "Where the fuck you come from, man?"

"I saw you when the BMW swung out of control down the street," Dante answered, as he stood staring down at the bleeding gunman. "Go get Natalie and get inside the SUV they left.

"What are you going to do?"

"I'ma be right behind you," Dante told him, as he was squatting down beside the bleeding gunman.

9

"Dominic, I'm worried!" Carmen told her husband, as she walked back and forth in front of her husband's desk, while he sat behind it quietly drinking a glass of brandy. "We've been waiting for almost three hours since we got back here. Where are they?"

In Spanish, Dominic told his wife that she needed to calm down and expressed that he was waiting to hear from them just as much as she was.

"But it's been . . ." Carmen stopped short hearing the knocking on her husband's office door.

"Come in!" Dominic yelled out.

"Mr. Saldana, sir!" Carlos said, as he stuck his head inside the office. "Dante's out front, sir, and he has both Natalie and Jonathan with him. Gomez is also with them, sir."

"Thank God!" Dominic said, just as his wife took off from the office.

Dominic left his office and followed his wife. Upon reaching the front door to their home, he saw his wife and daughter embrace. Dominic shifted his eyes out to where both Dante and Gomez were talking with Carlos, while standing next to a pearl-white Porsche with an SUV parked behind it.

"Daddy, you should have seen Dante," Natalie told her father, raising her head to look up at him. "He was really amazing when he showed up to help us."

"Was he now?" Dominic asked, as he held his daughter. He saw Carmen walk up the walkway with her arms wrapped around Dante's waist.

"I hear you were really amazing, Dante," Dominic told him, holding his bodyguard's eyes.

"I was just doing my job," Dante replied.

Gomez then walked up and said, "Mr. Saldana, sir. I don't know where you've found this guy but what I saw him do tonight was unbelievable. It's like he just appeared out of nowhere and was...I don't know how to explain it, sir."

Nodding his head, Dominic looked back at Dante as Carmen laid her head on his chest and hugged him.

Dominic said to his bodyguard, "I won't forget this, Dante. I am grateful to you for bringing my daughter back to us."

"Just doing my job," Dante answered again, but then added, "And just so you're aware. We don't just have Victor Fayman to deal with. We also have to deal with the same guy we've talked about before. Stevens!"

"How do you know it was Stevens?" Dominic asked, balling up his face as he stared hard at Dante.

"Come on, Natalie," Carmen spoke up. "Let's go and make sure Jonathan is doing alright."

"Natalie looked back to Dante as she followed alongside her mother. She watched Dante speaking with her father, as both Carlos and Gomez stood by. Natalie then caught Dante's eyes and smiled after receiving a quick wink of the eye he shot her before focusing back on her father.

After listening to Dante tell him about the dying gunman's confession, Dominic spoke up once Dante had finished: "I want Stevens taken care of. I have $200,000 for you once he is dead."

Nodding his head, Dante replied, "Just give me the information on him and I'll take care of 'em."

* * *

"Natalie! Mrs. Saldana!" Jonathan said as soon as both mother and daughter walked into the sitting room. He stood up from the sofa hc was relaxing on. "Is everything . . .?"

"Everything is fine, Jonathan!" Carmen told him, holding up her hand for Jonathan to relax. "Dante has taken care of everything."

"Dante?" Jonathan repeated, staring at Carmen and then Natalie with a confused look on his face.

"I will let my daughter explain who Dante is, Jonathan," Carmen told him, before turning to Natalie and saying, "I'll make the call to Jonathan's parents. I'll leave you to talk with Jonathan."

Nodding her head in understanding, Natalie stood watching her mother walk away before she slowly turned and faced Jonathan, as he asked, "Natalie, what the hell happened back there? Are you alright?"

"I'm fine, Jonathan," Natalie replied, looking down as Jonathan took her hands into his. She looked up to meet his eyes again, saying after a moment, "Jonathan, look! There is something I need to tell you."

"Wait!" Jonathan spoke up. "Let me go first. There's something I need to tell you before you say anything. First, I need you to know that I love you, Natalie. After what happened tonight, I'm sure that I can't see myself living without you and I want to ask you to marry me."

"What?" Natalie cried in disbelief, just as Jonathan kissed her directly on the lips.

"I'll give you two sometime alone," Dante's voice said, as Natalie pulled away from Jonathan and swung around to see Dante turning and walking away.

"Dante, wait!" Natalie cried, jumping up from beside Jonathan who then grabbed her hand and pulled her back down beside him.

"Natalie, did you just hear what I said? " Jonathan asked her smiling. "I want you to marry me."

Shaking her head, Natalie pulled her hands away from Jonathan and said, "Jonathan, I'm sorry. I can't marry you. I'm interested in someone else. And to be truthful with you, I think it's best if we stop seeing each other. I'm sorry!"

Jumping up from beside Jonathan, Natalie ran off to look for Dante, leaving Jonathan staring after her with a hurt and confused expression on his face.

* * *

At his new place standing out back next to the pool, Dante stood listening to the line ringing as he returned Vanessa's call.

"Hello!"

"Nessa! This Dante."

"Hey, big bruh! What's up?"

"Nothing really. You hit me up earlier. What's up?"

"I was calling from Angela's house. She been waiting for you to call. She keep saying she wants to talk to you about something."

"What she say it's about?"

"Something about what you and her talked about before you left. What's going on with you, though? How you like it there?"

Hearing his name from back inside the house, Dante started walking into the guesthouse. He told Vanessa to hold on as he stepped inside the patio's back entrance door, just as Natalie came rushing at him.

"Dante, I need to talk to you," Natalie told him in a rush, stopping in front of him and staring at him.

"Natalie, what's up? What's happened?"

"It's not that, Dante. I need to talk to you about something personal between me and you."

"What?" Dante said confused. "What you talking about, Natalie?"

"Dante, I know we only just met but I want us to get to know each other. I'm attracted to you and really want us to give things a chance between us."

"Whoa!" Dante said surprised. "Natalie, I work for your father and . . ."

"Dante, listen!" Natalie cut him off. "I don't care who you work for, whether it be my father or the governor. I want what I want, and it's you I want. Are you going to give me what I want?"

Dante watched Natalie walk away without waiting for a response. She didn't even look back at him as she walked out the front door. Dante shook his head as he walked back outside onto the patio.

"Shit just keeps getting crazy," Dante said to himself. Then he remembered he was still on the phone with Vanessa. "Nessa! You still there?"

"Mhm!" Vanessa answered, "I'm still here. And I see you still got the girl's going crazy even in Arizona."

"It ain't even like that."

"Who was that?"

"That was the daughter of the dude I work for."

"She sounded like she was serious just now, Dante. What's wrong with her?"

"Didn't I just tell ya she's the daughter of the nigga I work for, Vanessa?" Dante asked. "How that looks, me kicking it with this dude's daughter?'

"What's wrong with it?" Vanessa asked. "From what I just heard that girl tell you, you're her man whether you know it or not."

"Whatever!" Dante said. "Go head and give Angela my number."

"Alright," Vanessa answered. "You should see D.J., Dante. You know his ass walking a little now and stay his ass in something. Mya just as bad, but she talking a lot better than D.J. is."

Smiling at the mention of his kids, Dante heard himself asking about Alinna.

"Alinna is doing Alinna, Dante," Vanessa told him

Understanding fully what Vanessa was telling him, Dante changed the conversation by announcing, "Dre and Tony T should be there soon."

"They should be here sometime tomorrow."

"Make sure Dre hit me up when he touch down and make sure you get Angela my number to call me, alright?"

"I got it, big bruh!" Vanessa answered. "I love you, Dante! Be safe out there, alright?"

"You too, Vanessa. I love you, too, lil sis!"

10

Dante heard his cell phone go off as he stood outside the front
of the mansion beside his Benz, waiting for both Carmen and
Natalie to come out so they could leave for the fundraising event
Natalie had mentioned three days before. He pulled out the phone
and was surprised to see Angela was on the other end.

"You finally got around to calling me, huh?" Dante asked,
answering the call from Angela.

"It almost sounds like you miss me, Dante."

"You would like that, wouldn't you?"

"I would love to see you, Papi," she told him. "I miss you,
Dante!"

"Yeah, I miss you too, Angela. But what's up? You said you
needed to talk to me about something," Dante questioned, as he
looked back at the front door. Hearing it open, he saw Carmen and
then Natalie walk out the door of the mansion.

Unable to help but notice how different Carmen looked in jeans
and dressed more laid back, Dante shifted his eyes over at Natalie.

"Damn!" Dante said without thinking. Natalie's body was 5'3",
slim but curvy, and 34C-24-34. She was wearing fitted jeans that
hugged her curves perfectly and a Dolce and Gabbana shirt that
showed the full print and outline of her perky 34C breasts.

Dante!"

Hearing his name and remembering Angela was on the phone,
Dante opened the back door to the Benz as Carmen walked up
smiling at him. "Yeah, Angela, I'm here!"

"Arc you busy?"

"Naw! I'm listening to you," Dante answered, looking back to Natalie as she moved up behind him to the passenger front door.

Shaking his head as he closed the back door behind Carmen, Dante turned to see Natalie was already inside the car. He walked around to the driver side.

"I hear you, Angela," Dante said again. As he was closing the driver's door, he heard Angela calling out to him again.

"Dante, what are you doing?" Angela asked him sounding somewhat upset.

"Angela! Just talk, all right! I'm listening to you."

Sucking her teeth, Angela said, "Anyways, do you remember when we last spoke about Captain Whitehead's son that was with the D.E.A.?"

"I'm listening."

"Well, I just found out from the Chief of Police that the D.E.A. has been on the case for a little more than almost a month from the week you left."

"What all you have on this guy?"

"I have enough."

"Hold on, Angela," Dante told her. He then looked from the road to the rear view mirror asking, "Carmen, do you or Dominic have a fax machine?"

"Of course, Dante," Carmen answered. "Would you like the fax number?"

"If it's okay?" Dante replied.

Dante listened as Carmen gave him the number, which he then relayed to Angela, explaining that he wanted her to fax the information to him about who the undercover D.E.A. guy was.

"It'll take me a little while to get everything and fax it to you, but once I get it, I'll send it all to you," Angela told Dante.

Thanking Angela, Dante asked her to call him back later explaining that he was in the middle of something.

"Who was that?" Natalie asked as soon as he hung up.

"A friend of mine from back home in Miami," Dante told Natalie. "She's a captain for the Miami-Dade Police Department."

"Is that the same captain you've told me about, Dante?" Carmen spoke up from the back seat.

Meeting Carmen's eyes for a moment, Dante refocused on the road again before saying, "Yeah! She's the same captain."

"Well, anyways," Natalie said, as she reached over taking Dante's right hand from the steering wheel in her left hand and intertwining their fingers. She then placed their hands in her lap and continued, "My best friend is going to be at the event today and she wants to meet my new boyfriend."

Cutting his eyes first to Natalie who was smiling at him, Dante shifted his eyes to the rearview mirror to find Carmen staring out the back seat window while showing a small smile on her lip.

* * *

Once they arrived at the banquet hall, they left the Benz with a valet. Dante allowed Natalie to hold his hand as he kept his eyes on Carmen while she smiled and spoke to other guests who were arriving.

Dante followed the women into the building where an even larger group stood. He was surprised to see them all playing fair and various competitive games. Dante followed Carmen as she fell in with a group of women, only for Natalie to pull him back over beside her and say, "Momma is fine, Dante. If she needs you, you will know."

Dante looked back at where Carmen was and saw that she was laughing and enjoying time with her group of women. Dante then allowed Natalie to lead him off further into the huge room while still making sure he could keep an eye on Carmen.

Two minutes later, Natalie released Dante's hand. He watched as she rushed over to hug a dark-skinned, Spanish female. Dante turned his attention back across the floor, spotting Carmen talking with a middle-aged white man.

"Dante!"

Looking back around after hearing his name, he met both Natalie and the female as they walked up to him smiling.

"Dante, this is my best friend, Mari Elysse."

"It's good to meet you, Mari," Dante said, as he shook her hand.

"Natalie, he is too gorgeous. I'm going to scream at how sexy he is. I'm jealous," Mari spit at Natalie in Spanish. But then in perfect English she said to Dante, "It's good meeting you, too, Dante. Natalie has not stopped telling me about you since the two of you met."

Smiling a smirk-like smile, Dante spoke in near perfect Spanish, "I've heard some about you as well, but I hope to get to know more about you...and thanks for the complement. You're really cute yourself."

With her mouth wide open in shock and embarrassment, Mari turned to a laughing Natalie and said, "Why didn't you tell me he could understand and speak Spanish, Natalie?"

"I didn't realize that you would try to talk about him in Spanish!" Natalie said. She continued laughing as she stepped beside Dante and wrapped her arms around his waist.

Rolling her eyes at Natalie, Mari looked back to Dante and said, "Dante, I'm asking you this now. Would you mind signing up for the all-male bidding that the women are having here? There are going to be at least 25 men that the women will have to choose from. They will be bidding on which man they want to dance with and have one kiss with."

"Is this for the fundraiser?" Dante asked.

Nodding her head yes, Mari asked again, "So will you do it, Dante?"

"Sure, I'll help out," Dante answered, receiving a smile from Mari just before she said that she would be right back.

"So, you're interested in kissing someone else, Dante?" Natalie asked, as she shifted and stepped in front of him.

Looking down to meet Natalie's eyes, Dante said, "I only agreed because I was helping your friend out."

"Well, I'm not worried," Natalie told him, as she reached up and wrapped her arms loosely behind his neck. "I will definitely be making sure no woman gets what belongs to me."

"Ummm…excuse me, you two!" Carmen said as she walked up, smiling at both her daughter and Dante.

"Everything alright, Carmen?" Dante asked, giving her his full attention.

"Everything is fine, Dante," she told him, smiling at how handsome he was. "Actually, I only wanted to ask you a favor."

"Whatever you need," Dante told her.

Explaining to Dante that there was a best bodyguard competition that was going on outside in the back, Carmen asked Dante if he minded competing for the fundraiser as a favor for her.

Nodding his head yes, Dante gave a small smirk and answered, "Sure, Carmen. Anything you want."

* * *

Natalie followed her mother and Dante outside to the backgrounds of the banquet facility. She saw an area covered in padded blue mats surrounded by a big boxing ring with white ropes. There were two muscular men fighting in the center.

"I'll be right back, Natalie, honey!" Carmen told her daughter, as she led Dante off. "I'm just going to go get Dante signed in."

Catching Dante's quickly wink at her, Natalie found herself smiling.

"What are you doing out here, Natalie?" Mari asked. "Where Dante?"

"My mom is getting him signed up to complete in the bodyguard competition," Natalie responded, as she stood watching the competition that was going on at the moment.

"Natalie, are you serious?" Mari asked, staring at her friend. "Your mother is really going to sign your bodyguard and boyfriend up to fight?"

Smiling as she looked over at Mari, Natalie calmly said, "Relax, Mari. Dante is . . ."

"Natalie!" Jonathan said, as he walked up next to her and received both girls attention.

"Jonathan, what are you doing here?" Natalie asked in surprise, turning to face him.

"You don't remember? You invited me!" he told her, only to look up and see Carmen Saldana walking up. "Mrs. Saldana. How are you?"

"Jonathan," Carmen replied. "What are you doing here? Are your parents here also?"

"No, ma'am," he answered. "Actually Natalie invited me to come."

Looking at her daughter in surprise, Carmen kept her comment to herself. She then handed over Dante's black-leather jacket and his shoulder holster and said, "Dante wants you to watch his things, Natalie."

"Hi, Mrs. Saldana!" Mari said, smiling at her best friend's mother.

"Hello, Mari!" Carmen replied. "Where are your parents?"

"My father is inside with some business friends, and my mother should be out here somewhere," Mari told Carmen, as she looked around for her mother.

"Ummm...Natalie," Jonathan said, lightly touching the side of her arm to get her attention, "can I talk to you for a moment, please?"

"Jonathan, if you want to talk to me, you can talk to me here and now. I'm waiting to see my boyfriend compete in this competition," Natalie told him bluntly, as she turned to stare at Jonathan.

Staring at Natalie a moment while speechless after hearing that her boyfriend was actually with her, Jonathan found his voice and asked, "You're really here with your...this new guy you're seeing?"

Natalie felt someone touch her shoulder. She turned around to see that it was her mother, who nodded her head towards the competition.

She turned around to see what her mother was motioning at. Women began whistling and calling our flirtatiously. Natalie broke out in a smile when she saw Dante walk out onto the blue mats in his black metallic Gucci jeans and a white Calvin Klein wife beater shirt that hugged his muscular upper chest. Even his hard six-pack stomach was easily visible.

Jonathan stared at the guy who he remembered from the other night after he and Natalie were shot at. He saw the smile on her face and asked, "You mean this is the guy you're seeing now, Natalie?"

Carmen looked at Natalie and then at Jonathan's facial expression. She looked back at her daughter who was caught up in watching Dante.

Carmen turned her focus back onto Dante as well. She was just in time to see him swiftly dodge and weave a combination that his opponent threw at him. In response, Dante threw and landed two solid body blows to the other fighter's mid-section, dropping him to a knee, with one hand holding his stomach and the other hand laid out flat on the ground.

"Jesus!" Mari said in both shock and surprise, as she stood watching the fighter shaking his hands that he no longer wanted to fight. "Did you guys see how fast Dante moved?"

Smiling even harder, Natalie continued staring at Dante, just as he turned and looked directly at her, winking with a smirk on his face.

11

Dante had quieted the crowd with three straight wins, only to be talked into one more match against a dark-haired, white young man about his same age. Dante found himself really getting into the match. His opponent was unable to recognize his fighting style, but he respected his skills as they really got into it with each other.

Finding himself knocked backwards, with his back hitting the mat, Dante reacted before his opponent caught on to what was happening. Kicking upwards in a spin-like kick that turned into a handstand, Dante came out of the handstand just as the other young man stepped into a back flip.

Dante rushed his opponent as he was coming out of his flip and landed a solid forearm into his chest, sending him stumbling backwards and down to the mat.

"Enough!" Dante's opponent said, waving his hand that he was finished. He rubbed his chest with his other hand and smiled at Dante.

Smirking, as he stepped over the loser, Dante offered his hand down to the young man, helping him up from the mat and then asked, "What's ya' name, homeboy?"

"James Grant!"

"Dante Blackwell!"

Shaking the white boy's hand, Dante left the mat along with James. They heard people in the crowd throwing comments their way.

"So, who you working with here?" Dante asked. "You doing bodyguard work, right?"

"Actually, I'm just closing security for the fundraising event today," James answered.

"So you just do security work them?" Dante asked, just as Natalie rushed up to him.

"Oh, my God, baby! You were amazing!" Natalie told Dante as she leaned up and kissed him on the lips, catching Dante off guard.

Staring down at Natalie a moment, Dante shifted and introduced James to Carmen when she walked up.

"It's good to meet you, James," Carmen said, as she shook his hand. "You're a really good fighter if you can actually handle our Dante."

"Thank you, ma'am," James replied.

"Please, call me Carmen."

Nodding his head in understanding, James looked to Dante and asked, "So, where you learn to fight like that from?"

"Friend of my father taught me back when I was young," Dante answered. Then he asked, "What style was that you was using just now?"

"Actually, it's a mixed style I put together," James replied. "When I was younger, my dad put in a lot of money to teach me Muay Thai. After learning that I took up aikido and I just kind of ended up mixing the two."

"That's bad dude," Dante replied smiling. "I like your style."

"Same here!" James replied, as he and Dante touched fists.

"Ummm...excuse me!" Mari spoke up. "Dante, I hate to interrupt but it's almost time for the bidding. If you want, you can use the bathroom upstairs and get cleaned up."

"I'll show him!" Natalie spoke up, smiling up at him.

"We'll talk some more after this bidding thing over with," Dante told James, allowing Natalie to lead him off back inside the building.

* * *

Following Natalie as she led him into the bathroom that looked as if it could belong inside Dominic and Carmen's mansion, Dante barely got fully into the bathroom when Natalie pushed him up against the closed bathroom door and was all over him.

Pushing Natalie gently back, he broke their kiss as Natalie cried in protest. Dante said, "Natalie, come on! We can't . . ."

"Don't say it, Dante!" she demanded, cutting him off. "I don't want to hear it about you working for my father or anything else. I want to be with you and I am so serious, Dante. What is it? Are you not attracted to me?"

"Come on, Natalie!" Dante said, as he walked around her and sat on the edge of the counter facing her. "Of course, I'm feeling you. That's not the problem at all. It's just that I'm dealing with something…or someone…back at home."

"You mean Alinna?"

Staring at Natalie in surprise, Dante asked, "How you know about Alinna?"

"Because I heard you talking about her twice with your sister, Vanessa."

"When?"

"The first time was when I caught you outside by the pool at the guest house after the shooting. You thought I left but I came back and heard you talking. The second time was yesterday when I heard you talking to someone named Dre. You said something about letting Alinna do Alinna and admitted that you was finished with her."

"You heard all that?"

Nodding her head yes, Natalie walked over to Dante, stopped directly in front of him, and said, "Dante, I know about your son and daughter and I know that the captain you was on the phone with earlier is your daughter's mother, but the two of you are not together. I have to be honest with you though. I'm really falling in love with you, Dante. I just want you to give us a chance. I'm not asking for much. You said you're attracted to me too, so please, Dante! Give us a chance!"

Natalie again went in for a kiss, which Dante allowed. He felt her wrap her arms around his neck and he returned her kiss. He then reached around gripping Natalie's soft ass and squeezed it, which caused her to moan while still kissing him.

* * *

Ten minutes later, they returned downstairs to find a large group of women crowding the main floor in front of the stage. Natalie led Dante through the crowd of women hearing whispers that grew louder. Natalie saw Mari and her mother off to the side, with a crowd of smiling women all focused on the dark-skinned guy on the stage.

"Where the hell . . . ?"

"When does Dante go up?" Natalie asked, cutting Mari off as she started to complain.

Sucking her teeth, Mari grabbed Dante's hand, pulling him away and leading him past the smiling and staring women.

"So, how did it go?" Carmen asked smiling, watching her daughter as Natalie stood smiling at Dante.

As she shifted her eyes from watching Dante to her mother, Natalie answered, "He said she was with someone else."

"You mean his son's mother?"

Nodding her head yes, Natalie replied, "He still loves her but he also admitted that he cares for me."

"So, I take it that you two have agreed to see each other then?"

Nodding her head yes with an even bigger smile on her face, Natalie broke eye contact with her mother and shifted her eyes to the stage just as the women in the crowd began screaming and yelling out.

Watching Dante being escorted out onto the stage by a slim and young-looking white woman, Natalie felt her cheeks begin hurting as she stood smiling from ear to ear. She watched her man just as the bidding began on Dante.

* * *

"Alinna, relax!" Alex told her, glancing from the road over to Alinna and noticing the nervous expression she had on her face.

Looking over at Alex as he reached over, taking her hand in his and intertwining their fingers, Alinna gave a small smile before turning her attention back outside her window.

Five minutes later, watching as Alex slowed the Cadillac in front of a royal blue and white house, he parked his vehicle. Alinna turned to look over at him and heard someone yell out Alex's name.

Swinging her head back around, Alinna locked in on Alex's younger sister as she rushed out the front door to the house, running to the car.

"Come on!" Alex said, releasing Alinna's hand and climbing out of the car.

Taking a deep breath and slowly releasing it, Alinna opened the car door and climbed out to meet Alex's baby sister.

"So, this is her?" Kim said with a smile, looking away from her brother to Alinna. "Alex said you was beautiful. I agree with him. You are!"

"Alinna, meet my little sister, Kimberly Williams," Alex introduced them, smiling at Alinna and then over at his sister.

Shaking Kimberly's hand, Alinna said, "It's good to finally meet you, Kimberly. Alex tells me a lot about you."

"Call me Kim!" she told Alinna. She took her hand and led her off. "Come! Let's talk while Alex goes to the back where my husband is."

* * *

Arriving back at the mansion a little after 5:00 p.m., Dante parked the Benz out front. As he was climbing out of the driver's seat, the passenger and back doors were opened by the mansion's personal valet.

Dante walked around the car and handed his keys to the young valet to park the car. He looked over at Carmen just as Natalie took his hand in hers. She said, "I'll leave you two to enjoy the rest of the day since my daughter just paid $4,500 for you, Dante."

Dante watched as Carmen walked off with a smile on her face. He shifted his eyes down to Natalie as she pulled his hand and led him to the front door.

"Where we going?"

"I feel like being alone with you!" Natalie replied and said nothing else. She kept smiling as she led him inside the mansion and straight over to the elevator.

As soon as the both of them stepped onto the elevator and the door began closing, Dante felt Natalie grip his shirt and push him up against the elevator's back wall.

Stepping into Dante, she pressed herself up against him. She slyly reached up and wrapped her arms around his neck; pulling him down as she raised her heard and met his lips in a kiss.

Natalie moaned again as she felt Dante grip her ass in both his hands. She was busy grinding her lower half against Dante's hard-on imprint of his manhood when he broke the kiss.

Whining in protest, Natalie asked, "Dante, what's wrong? Why are you stopping?"

Reaching around her and hitting the open door button on the elevator control board, Dante caught the door before it closed again. He looked back at Natalie as she was turning to look at him and said, "I think we on our floor."

Smiling as she took his hand again, Natalie walked to the left after exiting the elevator toward a cream-colored hallway. Dante could hear the sound of her heels clicking against the tile floor.

At the end of the hallway she turned right toward two brown, oil-shined doors. Natalie led Dante into the professional home theater that her father had built.

"You joking, right?" Dante said in disbelief, staring around the huge room as he noticed the brown sofa-like theater seats.

"Come sit down!" Natalie told him smiling. She led Dante over to the wide and soft-cushioned sofa, pushing him down. "I'll be right back."

Watching Natalie as she walked away, Dante looked back at the wide theater screen, slowly shaking his head and smirking.

The lights went out after a few moments and a movie began to play on the screen. Dante was staring at the screen when he caught the strong smell of weed just as Natalie walked in front of him holding two bottles and a joint hanging between her lips.

"You smoke?" Dante asked, taking the bottle she handed him.

"Sometimes," Natalie answered, as she took the joint and placed it back between her lips and took a deep pull.

Surprised, Dante shook his head and turned his attention to the screen. When he saw Wesley Snipes, he recognized the movie was Art of War.

"Here!" Natalie said, handing Dante the joint. She took his beer bottle and sat it down next to hers atop the glass coffee table in front of them. Turning back to him, Natalie climbed onto his lap and straddled him. She bent down and took in the smoke he blew out, inhaling his hit before releasing the smoke.

She bent again to kiss Dante's lips as she reached down and undid his jeans, pulling down the zipper and lifting herself up a little. She reached inside and pulled out his semi hard-on from his boxers.

"Oh, my God!" Natalie cried in disbelief and shock as she stared down at the size and thickness of Dante's manhood.

"Oh! So what, you scared now?" Dante asked, as he held the joint up to his lips, taking in another deep pull.

Feeing how nervous she truly was now but not willing to admit it, Natalie slowly smiled as she began pulling off her shirt. She had never been more aroused in her life.

* * *

"Oh...my...God!" Natalie said, bravely getting her words out over her deep breathing after having three unbelievable orgasms.

She took his too thick, too fat, and too long manhood inside her, even though a few inches couldn't fit.

Brushing back her hair and smiling when Natalie met his eyes, Dante asked, "You alright?"

Nodding her head yes while smiling down at Dante, Natalie bent to kiss him as she began moving up and down on his manhood.

"Oh God, Dante! Baby, you feel so…yessss! That feels so good!" Natalie moaned, as she rode Dante, feeling him pushing deeper into her.

Dante listened to her as she dug her nails into his shoulders where she gripped him. He watched her face as her eyes rolled to the back of her head as her pussy muscles worked and she came on his dick. He held her body as she shook in his arms again crying out his name.

Waiting until she calmed down, Dante lightly slapped Natalie on the ass and said, "Get up!"

Doing as she was told, she climbed off of Dante, allowing him to position her on the sofa facing the back. On her knees, Natalie looked over her shoulder watching as Dante stepped up behind her.

"God, yes!" Natalie cried, as Dante pushed back inside her. "Baby, slow. Go slow, baby, please!"

Doing as she asked, he worked himself slowly inside her, until his whole manhood was buried deep inside. He leaned forward against her back and listened to the way she was breathing. He kissed her neck and whispered into her ear, "You know I'm all the way inside, right?"

Nodding her head yes, she was unable to speak. Natalie gripped the back of the sofa with her nails sunk in as she felt Dante begin moving inside of her.

"So this what you wanted, huh?" Dante asked, as he slowly pushed in and out of Natalie. Seeing her nod her head, he said, "I need you to answer me. Say something!"

"Yes! Yes, baby!" Natalie called out.

Dante smiled as he pushed a little deeper. As he heard her cry out his name, he asked, "So, tell me. Who does this pussy belong to?"

"It's…it's yours, Dante!" Natalie cried. "It's yours and I'm all yours, baby! Oh, God! I love you!"

"Good answer," Dante replied, smiling. He leaned back as he gripped her nipples while pushing deeper and a little faster inside of her. He listened to the sound of his name as Natalie cried out to him.

12

Trailing behind Stevens for the second day after receiving information on the heroin king pin dealer, Dante's phone went off. He picked it up and answered, "Yeah!"

"Hey, baby! You busy?"

"What's up, Natalie?"

"Where you at?'

"Taking care of something. Everything alright?"

"When are you coming home?"

"What's up, Natalie? What's the problem?"

"Who said there was as problem? I just wanted to know when you was coming home. I miss you!"

"You miss me, huh?" Dante repeated, shaking his head and smirking as he slowed the Benz after seeing Stevens limo turn down a side street. "Baby, look. Let me call you back."

"Dante, wait!"

"Yeah!"

"Can we go out with Mari and her friend tonight? Daddy already said that he isn't going anywhere tonight."

"I knew you wanted something. Let me call you back with the answer," Dante told her, hanging up the phone.

After parking up the street from the corner where Stevens limo turned, Dante climbed out of the Benz and hit the remote locks as he began jogging up the street.

Feeling his cell phone wake up as it vibrated in his pocket, Dante dug the thing out while continuing up the street. He saw that the limo was parked in front of a warehouse.

"Yeah!" Dante answered, without looking to see who was calling.

"Hey, big bruh!"

"Vanessa, what's up?'

"Same thing as always. I was calling to see if you was coming down for the birthday party we're throwing for Alinna this Saturday."

"Why would I come?" Dante asked, as he stared at the warehouse from up the street, wondering what was inside the building.

"Dante, come on!" Vanessa said, breaking his train of thought. "Alinna's still your son's mother and no matter what you two are going through she still loves you. And I know you still love her."

"What's that gotta do with me coming to this party though?"

"Alright! Do it for me then. Come to the party because I miss you and want to see you."

Sighing deeply, Dante noticed the warehouse door open as Stevens and six of his security guards walk out. Each guard was holding a black duffel bag.

"Alright, Vanessa. I'ma come for you."

"Be here early Saturday so you can spend some time with D.J. and Mya."

"Yeah, alright!"

"Thank you and I love you."

"I love you, too, Vanessa."

* * *

Dante returned to his Benz, driving off while Stevens' limo drove off in the opposite direction. Then he made a phone call.

"Saldana!" Dominic answered after two rings.

"Dominic. This Dante."

"Dante! Is everything okay?"

"Yeah!" Dante answered. He asked, "Tell me something. Do you know where Stevens keeps the shipments he picks up?"

"Actually, no!" Dominic answered. "Stevens is pretty quiet and extra careful in keeping that information unknown to others."

"Well, I think I may have found the location," Dante told his employer. "I'ma tell you more about it when I get back to the mansion. I've also got an idea how I'ma take care of this Stevens problem and come up with added product."

"Whatever you have to do to handle this issue, do it!" Dominic told Dante. "We have nothing to discuss, Dante. Do what you will!"

Hearing Dominic hang up the phone, Dante then hung up his car phone. Remembering something, he picked his phone up out again, looked up a number, and made a call.

"Hello?"

"James, what's up? This Dante!"

"Dante. What's up, man?"

"Yo, tell me something, J! You handling something right now?"

"Like what?" James asked confusedly. "What you talking about, Dante?"

"Check me out! I got some work I can use you on. You interested?"

"Don't even think twice about it. What's up? What we handling?"

"Whoa!" Dante said stopping the white boy. "This shit I'm talking about ain't none of that security work you be into. This shit I'm talking about likely to get stupid."

"I'm not stupid, bro. I know I'm a white boy but I'm not your normal kinda white guy. I know about Dominic Saldana and the type of business he is into. I'm still interested. When is the job supposed to be?"

Loving the vibe that James was giving off, Dante said, "Alright! Meet me at this address in ten minutes. Grab a pen and some paper."

Giving James the address to Dominic's mansion, Dante hung up and then called the mansion and spoke with Carlos, giving him a heads up. He explained that a while guy named James Grant would be showing up at the mansion and that he was a friend of his.

Hanging up with Carlos, Dante drove back to the mansion. He found his mind drifting back to his conversation with Vanessa and Alinna's birthday party.

* * *

Making it to the mansion a little while later, Dante nodded to the security at the front gate as he drove inside and drove his Benz up to the front of the mansion, as the valet waited.

He parked the car and climbed out, leaving it running for the valet. He then walked up to the front door just as the mansion's head maid opened it with a smile.

"Mr. Blackwell, sir! You have a guest for you inside the den being accompanied by Mr. Saldana," she told Dante as he stepped inside the house.

Dante thanked the maid and headed towards the den, where he could hear laughter. He walked in to see both Natalie and James seated together on the sofa.

"Dante!" James said, standing up as soon as Dante walked into the den.

"What's up, James?" Dante replied, as Natalie jumped up from the sofa and rushed to him.

"Hi, baby!" Natalie cried happily, throwing her arms up around Dante's neck to kiss him on the lips.

Breaking the kiss after a moment, Dante met her eyes saying, "Miss me, huh?"

Nodding her head, Natalie kissed Dante again and said, "I'ma wait for you at your place."

Dante watched as Natalie left the den after saying goodbye to James. Dante shook his head smirking as he turned back to his guest.

"You're a luck dude, man," James told Dante with a smile. "She's been talking about you since I got here."

"How long you been here?" Dante asked, as he and James sat down back on to the sofa.

"Not that long," James answered. "I talked with Carmen as well."

Nodding his head, Dante asked, "Tell me something, James. You know who Stevens Collmen is?

"Stevens Collmen? Who doesn't?"

"So you know what type of dude he is then?"

"What would you say if I told you I actually did some work for Stevens Collmen?" James asked, staring at Dante with a smile on his lips.

Staring back at James a few moments, Dante finally spoke up: "J, no bullshit! You did some work for this clown?"

"Yeah!" James answered. "I did some security work for him when he was handling some type of business deal with a guy named Victor something."

"Whoa!" Dante said, sitting forward and turning toward James. "What you say that other name was again?"

"Victor . . ." James replied.

He sat thinking for a moment until Dante asked, "Was it Victor Fayman?"

"That's it!" James answered, smiling. "That's what the name was. Black guy named Victor Fayman."

Dante slowly smiled as an idea popped into his head. He then stood up and said, "Come on! I want you to meet Dominic Saldana."

* * *

While Dominic felt a little uncomfortable allowing a stranger into his house, he allowed the meeting to happen only because of his trust in Dante. Still, he still made sure that Carlos was also a part of the meeting.

Listening as the young man began explaining about his security detail, Dante found himself sitting forward at the mention of Stevens Collmen's name and the fact that the young white man had done security work for him.

"Hold it!" Dominic said after the mention of Victor Fayman's name and the fact that both Stevens and Victor had met on a business deal together: "You're saying that both Victor Fayman and Stevens Collmen are business associates?"

"Yes, sir!" James answered. "I've witnessed two other meetings between Victor Fayman and Stevens Collmen."

"Have you been to Stevens' mansion?" Carlos asked, drawing James' attention to him.

"I've never been to his mansion," James continued, "but I have been to his penthouse out on the beach."

"Can you remember how to get there?" Dante asked, drawing the attention back to him.

"Sure!" James answered him.

Looking back at Dante and seeing the look on his face, Dominic held up his hand and said, "There's nothing more we need to discuss, Dante. Do what you will and let me know once it's done."

Nodding his head in understanding, Dante looked at Carlos and said, "I need some toys for me and my boy, James, here. You think you can help me out?"

"Whatever they need, make sure that they have it, Carlos!" Dominic told his head of security. He then stood up and continued, "I will not be leaving to go anywhere tonight. Mrs. Saldana wishes to remain at home. I do not want to be interrupted unless it is very important, gentlemen."

Leaving Dominic's office, Dante led James outside and began walking around the grounds surrounding the mansion.

"So, what's up, man?" James said, after a few minutes. "What's the plan?"

Glancing over toward James, Dante said, "James, look! You was right about you not being the average white boy. I agree with that but I'ma ask you this one more time before we go any further. You sure you trying to get tied up in this shit that's about to go down?"

"My answer still hasn't changed," James told Dante, looking over to him. "I'm still with you. So what's the plan?"

Nodding his head slowly, Dante said, "Alright! We handling this tonight. Understand though that this is only part one of our plans."

"I'm with you bro!" James replied, reaching over and touching fists with Dante.

13

"Why?

"We got something to handle."

"So, I guess that means we're not going out with Mari and your new friend then?"

Hearing the way she sounded, Dante's eyes moved from the clothes he was thumbing through in his closet over to Natalie's face. He signed deep and walked over and sat beside her.

"Look Natalie, I gotta do this because it's what your father pays me to do. How about you call Mari and have her and her friend come here and we can watch a movie up in the theater. When James gets here, I'll leave and handle this issue. Then, when I get back we can all go out to a club or grab something to eat. How you feel about that?"

"How long will you be gone?" Natalie asked, still pouting.

"I'll try to be back under an hour," Dante answered, holding Natalie's eyes.

Shaking her head, Natalie said, "Try to get back here sooner than an hour, Dante. Please."

"I'ma try!" Dante told her, winking his eye. She returned with a smile and kiss.

Dante returned to picking out an outfit to wear that night. He selected black jeans, a black t-shirt, a cotton hoody sweat suit, and a pair of black steel-toed boots.

Then he picked out a Gucci outfit to wear after he and James finished up with their business and he could head out with Natalie and Mari. Dante then jumped into the shower with Natalie joining him moments later.

Not surprised that he and Natalie ended up going at it as soon as the shower door closed, Dante spent the next fifteen minutes holding Natalie up mid-air as she rode him. This caused her to scream through two orgasms. After switching positions, she climaxed three more time until Dante finally released his seed deep inside her, while tightly gripping her hips. She smiled back at him over her shoulder as he leaned in and laid his face in the crack of her neck. She whispered, "I love you, Dante."

* * *

Once Mari and her new friend Edwin arrived at the mansion, Dante allowed Natalie to lead them up to the theater. Dante was stuck with Edwin when they reached the theater, since Mari and Natalie left to go pick out which movie they would watch. Dante listened to homeboy talking but cut his eyes over to him when he mentioned how sexy Natalie was.

"Here, baby!" Natalie said, handing Dante a beer as she and Mari walked back out to join Dante and Edwin.

Thanking Natalie, as she sat down in his lap, Dante leaned back in the sofa. Natalie made herself comfortable in his lap just as the lights went out and the movie began to play.

Dante missed the name of the movie as he felt Natalie slide her hand down to grip his manhood. She felt his dick hardening as she stroked and caressed him through the black jeans he was going to be wearing out with James.

"Watch the movie, Natalie!" Dante whispered, grabbing her hand and stopping her from what she was doing.

Hearing Natalie whine as her face balled up in the dim light, Dante couldn't help smile at how spoiled she was. So he wrapped his arms around her waist, kissed her neck, and whispered, "You know you my baby, right?"

Smiling at his words and looking back into his eyes, Natalie kissed him and said, "I love you too, Dante."

* * *

Excuse me, Mr. Blackwell!" Dante and Natalie both heard the maid say as she walked up beside them.

"Yeah! What is it?" Dante asked, staring past Natalie at the middle-aged maid.

"You have a guest waiting for you downstairs, sir," the maid said softly.

Thanking the maid, Dante shifted his attention to Natalie only to find her staring straight at him.

"Remember, you promised me," Natalie reminded him, climbing off of his lap.

"What's wrong, you two?" Mari asked, looking over at both of them.

"Dante needs to handle something and then he'll be right back," Natalie explained before walking with Dante out of the theater and into the hallway.

"You alright?" Dante asked, reaching up and brushing her hair out of her face.

Nodding her head, Natalie said, "Just be careful, Dante, and come back. Please!"

"I promise!" Dante told her, winking his eye and kissing her before turning and walking off.

Stopping off at the guesthouse to pick up his guns, Dante walked back to the front of the mansion, where James and Carlos were talking out on the front porch.

"What's up, fellas?" Dante spoke up, causing both Carlos and James to turn around.

"You tell me!" James replied, touching fists with Dante. "You ready?"

"Yeah!" Dante answered, as Carlos bent down and picked up a black leather duffel bag.

"This what you ask for?" Carlos asked Dante, handing him the bag.

Nodding his head and taking the bag, Dante looked to James and asked, "You got that?'

"It's parked next to your car," James replied, nodding his head towards the garage.

Nodding his head to James, Dante said, "Alright! Let's get this over with."

* * *

Seated in the driver's seat of the U-Haul truck, James drove away from the mansion. Dante sat looking inside the duffel bag to make sure he had all the stuff he had asked for.

"Where this place at, bro?" James asked, glancing over at Dante.

After giving James directions to the warehouse, Dante remembered the trip he had agreed to make back home. He asked, "What you doing this weekend?"

"Nothing really," James answered. "Why?"

"You wanna roll down south with me?" Dante asked. He explained, "I'm supposed to head back home to Miami for a few days if you wanna roll?"

"Hell yeah!" James answered smiling. "I never been to Miami. When we leaving?"

"Be ready Friday morning by five o'clock," Dante told him, as he thought about the trip back home and how everybody was going to react to seeing him.

Deep in thought, Dante snapped out of it when James called out to him that they were at their location.

"Stop over there!" Dante told James, pointing towards the building with a sign that read Arizona Plastic Co. "We walking up to the warehouse."

Climbing from the U-Haul truck, both of them were happy to find the business closed and the parking lot empty. Dante snatched up his duffel bag and closed the passenger door.

Walking around the back of the truck to meet James, Dante nodded for James to follow him and then asked, "You strapped?"

"I got a lil something," Dante heard James answer as he lifted up his shirt showing a .38 snub nose.

Pulling the banger from his back, Dante flipped the .45 automatic around with the handle facing James and said, "Take this!"

"What about you?" James asked, taking the gun from him.

"I'm good!" Dante replied, smirking.

They made it to the warehouse and noticed there were no vehicles in sight. They could, however, hear noises coming from inside the building the closer they got. Dante held his finger up to his lips for James to be quiet and then whispered, "We not gonna just walk straight through the front door. Walk around back and see if you can find another opening into the warehouse. Text me if you can."

As he watched James jog off and disappear into the darkness, Dante turned his attention back to the warehouse. He was staring at the top level of the building when he noticed headlights and then caught the sound of an approaching vehicle.

Taking off into the darkness, while pulling his second banger from the front of his jeans, Dante laid his back against the side of the warehouse as he listened to the wheels of the vehicle pull up. He peeked around the side and smiled at seeing Stevens and two other guys in suits. They were getting out of the same limo he saw him in earlier, noticing more security than before.

"What the fuck is going on out here now?" Dante said to himself. Then he froze at catching the sound of footsteps. It was too late, though, as a gun was placed against the back of his head.

"Move and I promise I'll open the back of your head!" the security threatened. He forcefully pushed Dante out from the darkness and called out to his boss.

* * *

Hearing his name, Stevens turned and looking around to his far right, he could see someone walking out of the darkness from the side of the building. He recognized the second person as one of his own men. He stood staring as both men walked closer to him. He began to slowly smile, recognizing the young man with the gold inside his mouth.

"Well, if it isn't Dominic's newly hired bodyguard," Stevens said, smiling harder once Dante stopped in front of him.

"I found him hiding over on the south side of the building," the security guard told his boss, gun still held at Dante's head.

Shifting his eyes back to Dante while still smiling, Stevens asked, "So tell me, how did you find this place out here in the middle of nowhere?"

"I got lucky!" Dante answered, staring hard straight at Stevens.

"Well, I guess your luck has run out tonight," Stevens said. He ordered the guard, "Take him up and lock him inside my office until I'm finished with Mr. Sutter."

"Get moving!" the guard told Dante, pushing him forward.

Dante walked to where he was told and entered the building through a side front door, while Stevens and the company he was with entered through the front double-sliding steel doors. Dante looked around and saw people carrying boxes and stacks and stacks of barrows all over the warehouse.

"Keep moving!" the security guard told Dante, shoving him forward again towards a set of steel steps.

"You do know I'ma kill you, right?" Dante asked him, as he made his way up the stairs.

"Shut the fuck up!" the guy told Dante, shoving him forward again, causing Dante to stumble.

Catching his balance while shooting homeboy a murderous look, Dante continued up the steps and followed directions. He then turned to walk toward the skybox-like office when he heard somebody ask, "Yo, Dante! You need some help?"

Spinning around at the sound of a voice, the guard stared at the white boy smiling at him. Just as he was about to ask who he was, a pain exploded from the side of his neck causing him to stagger.

Following the forearm he slammed into the guard's neck, Dante caught him before he dropped to the ground, as he twisted and broke his neck. He gently laid him on the ground.

"What the fuck took you so long?" Dante whispered, as he picked up both the guard's gun and the duffel bag that he had taken from him.

"I was waiting for the right time," James said, watching Dante pull another gun from the dead guard's pants.

"Right time, huh?" Dante said, shooting James a look as he tossed the duffel bag strap around his left shoulder and neck. "Whatever, but listen to this . . ."

"I already know," James said, as Dante pulled out a MAC-11 from inside the duffel bag and handed it over to him. "I saw Stevens outside. Where the hell did you come from?"

"You know how to use one of them, right?" Dante asked, while pulling a Tec-9 from the duffel bag for himself.

"Yeah! I got this," James answered. "What's the plan now?"

"Just follow my lead!" Dante told him, nodding for James to follow behind him.

* * *

Stevens walked with his new potential buyers, showing them the barrows he had packed with heroin at the bottom while Dixie Crystal sugar bags aligned the top for safer transport. Stevens watched Mr. Sutter and his entourage examine the heroin when the shooting started.

"What in the hell?" Stevens yelled, spinning around to see his security team being shot down.

"What's going on here?" Mr. Sutter yelled to Stevens over the shooting.

Stevens watched as his men were being gunned down, before turning his attention to the young black man with the semi-automatic gun in his hand. He was insanely walking out onto the main floor and firing his gun while killing more of his men. Stevens caught the expression in the young man's eyes at the same time he let a burst of bullets go from his gun. Running out of ammo, he dropped the gun and snatched two more from his waist. He opened fire again on two more of Stevens' men who ran up on him.

"What the hell! Who is this guy?" Stevens said.

* * *

As Stevens and his goons make a run for the door, Dante broke off in a sprint. He ended up sliding to a quick stop before stepping into a kick that slammed into the knee of one of the men that rushed at him.

Dante quickly dealt with two more men before putting a bullet into the guy's head whose knee he had just broken. He took off outside, finding James standing over Stevens and his remaining associates pointing his MAC-11 at the three of them.

"What the fuck took you so long?" James asked, cutting his eyes over to Dante and then back at Stevens and his friends.

14

Clearing out as many of the sugar barrows as the U-Haul truck could hold, they left Stevens Collmen and his men inside the burning warehouse after releasing Stevens' two business associates with the understanding of what I.O.U. meant. Dante sat inside the passenger seat listening to the phone ring as he called Dominic's private line while smoking one of his Black & Mild's.

Dante apologized for interrupting Dominic and Carmen's evening as he explained that he had the heroin from Stevens' warehouse and needed directions to where to go drop the stuff off.

Dante hung up from Dominic and repeated the directions to James. Then he called Natalie.

"Who is this?" Natalie answered the phone.

"Whoa! What's wrong with you?" Dante asked, surprised how she answered the phone.

"Dante, where the hell are you?"

"Alright, hold up!" Dante told her, stopping the whole conversation. "How about we start over and you tell me your problem, Natalie."

Dante listened as Natalie told him about Mari's supposedly new friend disrespecting her by trying to touch and flirt with her when Mari left the room to use the bathroom. Dante interrupted asking, "Where he at now?"

"I had Carlos escort him out."

"Alright! I'ma be there in a few minutes."

Hanging up with Natalie, Dante told James about Mari's friend and what Natalie told him had happened.

Turning his attention out of his window after telling James what happened and thinking about the comment Edwin made earlier, Dante nodded his head yes at hearing James ask if the girls were OK.

Once they arrived at the storage location, Carlos was waiting with a team of security. Dante also saw Dominic's Bentley parked between two Range Rovers.

He climbed out of the U-Haul once James parked and shut the front door. Carlos walked over and opened up the back door of the Bentley as a smiling Dominic stepped out.

"Dante!" Dominic said, still smiling as he walked over to him. "I assume that after what was said over the phone that Stevens Collmen will no longer be a trouble to us?"

"Mr. Saldana, sir!" Carlos called out from the back of the U-Haul.

Looking back, Dante was smiling again as Dominic said, "Let's see what the two of you have brought me."

Following alongside James as Dominic led the way to the back of the truck, Dante stood as Dominic and Carlos marveled at all the sugar barrows packed inside the back of the truck.

"I'm not sure how much heroin is inside each barrow, but there are bags of real sugar on the top," Dante explained. "No disrespect, Dominic, but I need to get back to the mansion."

Nodding his head hardly listening to what Dante had just told him. Still struck by the amount of goods they had stolen, Dominic looked to both James and Dante and said, "Very well done, Dante and Mr. Grant."

"Not a problem, sir!" James replied, with a slight nod of the head.

When Carlos whispered something to Dominic, Dante shifted his eyes over to Dominic's face. He saw his expression change immediately before he looked over at Dante.

"Is everything alright?" Dominic asked, balling his face up a little.

"It will be," Dante replied, with a serious expression on his face.

"I trust that it will," Dominic said, his smile returning. "I have a car for the two of you to use to get back to the mansion."

"Thanks!" Dante replied, as Carlos handed him a set of keys.

Breaking off from Dominic and Carlos, the two headed over to the metallic black BMW M3. Dante tossed the keys over to James and instructed, "You driving!"

* * *

They made it back to the mansion in about 20 minutes; especially with the way James was working the BMW's stick shift. Dante hopped from the car as soon as James parked out front.

Running upstairs, with James right behind him, Dante shot past the head maid as she held the door for the two of them.

Dante took the stairs two at a time to the second floor, taking a left at the top and sprinting down the hallway.

Pushing open the theater doors, he found the room to be empty. Dante then dug out his cell phone and called Natalie.

"Hello!"

"Natalie, where you at?"

"Baby, I'm in the guest house. What's the . . . ?"

Hanging up the phone, Dante called to James as he took off back towards the stairs, shooting back down to the bottom floor and jogging towards the guesthouse.

"Natalie!" Dante yelled, as he snatched open the front door to his place.

"Dante!" Natalie called, as she rushed from the kitchen. Seeing both Dante and James, she said, "Baby, what's wrong? What's happened, Dante?"

"You okay?" Dante asked, as he grabbed Natalie, looking her over.

"Dante, I'm . . ." Realizing what was wrong with her man, Natalie broke out in a smile as she wrapped her arms around his waist, laying her head against his chest. "You was worried about me?"

"Of course, I was worried about you!" Dante realized Mari was standing at the kitchen's breakfast bar watching them, as he looked over Natalie's head.

Releasing Natalie, Dante walked over to Mari. He dropped his arms across her shoulder and asked, "You alright, shorty?"

Nodding her head yes, Mari leaned into Dante apologizing for causing trouble.

"You good, Mari!" Dante told her. "How about we continue with what we planned."

"Dante, it's only three of us though," Natalie spoke up.

"Naw!" Dante replied, looking over to James. "What's up, J? You feel like going out with us tonight? You can hold down Mari tonight."

"I'm cool with it, if Mari is cool with it," James said, looking from Dante to Mari.

"So what's up, baby girl?" Dante asked, looking back to Mari. "We going out or what?"

* * *

Hearing her phone start to ring as she and Alex lay together, Alinna snatched it up quickly, answering it before it could wake Alex from his sleep. "Yeah!"

"What's up, Alinna? Remember me, bitch?"

"What? Who this?"

"Oh, you can't remember now, huh? Well, let's take a trip down memory lane," the voice told her laughing lightly. "Remember the last time you and I met, your last words were that 'this was your city and that business between us wasn't gonna happen?'"

"How the fuck did you get my number, bitch-ass nigga? What the fuck do you want?" Alinna said angrily, realizing whom she was talking to.

Laughing over the line after hearing Alinna recognize who he was, the voice said, "I'll let you get back to you rest with your new husband, since I'm sure the two of you been at each other since you entered homeboy's condo. I guess it's true what everybody says after all. Dante saw what type of bitch you are and left your ass. But I tell you what. I'll offer you a deal this time. Come work for me and maybe I'll let you taste this dick from time to time. Think about it!"

Hearing the phone hang up, Alinna crawled out of bed naked, left the bedroom, and called Vanessa.

"Yeah?" Vanessa answered half asleep after three rings.

"Vanessa, wake up!"

"What. Who this?"

"Nessa, this Alinna! Wake up, bitch! We got problems to handle."

"Hold on!" Vanessa told Alinna.

Peeking back inside the bedroom at Alex to make sure he was still asleep, Alinna focused back on the phone call, hearing Vanessa call her name.

"Yeah! Yeah! I'm right here."

"Alright! So what's going up that you had to call and wake me up at three in the morning?"

"You not gonna believe who just called my phone, Vanessa."

"Who?"

"Stupid-ass Fish Man!"

"You talking about that dude we got into it with some months back who wanted to do business with us?"

"The same muthafucker!" Alinna replied. "This muthafucker got the nerve to offer me a deal to work for his punk ass. He also mentioned Dante and that we're not together no more."

"How the hell he know that?" Vanessa asked. "Where the fuck his ass been hiding at?"

"I have no idea but I'ma find out where his ass at and deal with 'em!" Alinna said. "Do me a favor! Talk to Wesley, have him talk to his people, and see what they can find out about Fish Man and get back to me."

"Where the hell you at?" Vanessa asked. Sucking her teeth, she continued, "Don't even worry about answering that. You with that nigga you messing with. Bye!"

* * *

Hanging up with Alinna and shaking her head, Vanessa turned to head back inside her and Dre's bedroom but stopped short when she had a thought.

Pulling up a number in her phone, Vanessa walked off from the bedroom to make a call.

"Hello!"

Hearing the female voice answer after four rings, Vanessa said, "Ummm…is this Dante's phone?"

"Mmm huh! Who's calling?"

"Who's this?"

"This is his girlfriend! Who's this?"

"Hold on! This Natalie?"

"This is! How do you know who I am? Who is this calling?"

"I'm sorry! This is Vanessa, Dante's . . ."

"You're Dante's sister!" Natalie cut in saying, "Dante talks about you a lot. How are you?"

"I'm okay," Vanessa answered. "Is Dante there?"

"He's actually asleep right now. We just got . . ."

"Who's that, Natalie?"

Hearing Dante's voice in the background, Vanessa heard Natalie tell him she was on the phone.

"What's up, Nessa?" Dante asked, as he came over the line a moment later.

"Hey, playboy! I see you went ahead and got with the girl, huh?"

"Yeah! What's up though, lil sis? Everything good?"

"Actually no!" Vanessa answered. She went straight into the story that Alinna had just told her about the phone call from their old friend, Fish Man.

"So, what? This fool still trying to cause some problems since Alinna ain't wanna fuck with 'em on a business level?" Dante asked, once Vanessa was finished explaining.

"That's what it sounds like," Vanessa answered.

Sighing deeply, Dante said, "Alright! I'ma leave and head back there. I'ma call you when I hit Miami."

"Alright! I'll let Angela know you'll be here since she been asking about you lately. Love you!" Vanessa hung up the phone, with a smile.

* * *

"Dante, you did not just say that you was leaving and going back to Miami?" Natalie angrily asked, as soon as he lowered the phone from his ear.

"Natalie, come on! You need to . . ."

"Do not tell me to relax, Dante!" Natalie shot back, cutting him off. "You're just going to agree to leave and run back to Miami without discussing this with me first?"

Sighing as he sat up in bed with Natalie angrily staring at him, he found himself explaining the problem his family was having back in Miami. He promised Natalie he would be back within two weeks.

"I wanna come with you!" Natalie told him.

"No, Natalie!" Dante told her, staring hard at her.

Ignoring the look on his face, Natalie replied, "I wasn't asking, Dante. I'm telling you I want to go."

"Natalie! Look! I hear what you saying, but I'm serious. You're not coming with me. I can't focus on what I'm supposed to be doing down there if I'm worried about you at the same time. Just stay here for me, Natalie."

Staring at Dante a few moments, she said softly, "Dante, promise me that you're not going down there because you want your kids mothers back. I mean either of them!"

Shaking his head as he reached over to brush her hair back, Dante leaned towards her and kissed her lips. He pulled back a little meeting her eyes and said, "Natalie, you have nothing to worry about. I'm yours. And I know I don't say it but I am in love with you. I swear it!"

Looking at Dante in complete shock and surprise, Natalie felt the tears sliding down her face as she wrapped her arms around his neck, kissing him as they both fell back against the bed together.

⚜ ⚜ ⚜

While Natalie slept after they made love, Dante began packing and made a call to James. He let him know the situation and his plans, relieved to hear James say that he would be to the mansion in an hour packed and ready to go.

Dante took a shower after packing his bags and got dressed in a black and cream-colored Louis Vuitton outfit and some brown Timberlands. Dante checked the time on his new Gucci watch with a Mickey Mouse face that had white and yellow diamonds around the face. He decided he wasn't waiting any longer to wake up Dominic.

Dante called Carlos and asked him to wake up Dominic and have them all meet in his office. Dante hung up with Carlos and woke up Natalie.

"Mmmm…yeah, baby?" Natalie asked, as she rolled over and sat up after seeing that Dante was already fully dressed and standing on her side of the bed. "You leaving?"

"Yeah!" Dante answered, as he walked around to the foot of the bed and bent down to pick up two black leather duffel bags. "Come walk me to the mansion."

Natalie climbed out of the bed in only panties and a bra. She slipped on one of Dante's t-shirts and then walked over to him and wrapped her arms around his left arm.

Heading from the guesthouse over to the mansion, they met up with Carlos in the hallway leading to Dominic's office. Dante nodded his head in response to hearing that James was inside the den waiting for him.

Dante arrived at Dominic's office and knocked on the door. He heard him tell him to come in. He told Natalie to let James know that he would be with him shortly and he entered the office.

"Dante, what seems to be the emergency?" Dominic asked, waving to the chair in front of his desk as he sat comfortably in his desk chair, arms folded.

Turning down the invitation to sit, Dane began, "Dominic, I wanted to let you know that I need to leave for a little while. My family is going through a serious problem and need my help. I shouldn't be gone longer than two weeks. But if something comes up and you need me, I will return with no questions asked."

"It is fine, Dante," Dominic told him with a smile. "After the issue with Stevens, I've heard that Victor has left Arizona. For the moment, things are how they should be. But if I need you, I will call. Tell me, though, how big is this problem your family is dealing with?"

"I'm really not sure!"

Nodding his head, Dominic looked at Carlos and said, "Carlos, I want ten of our men ready in thirty minutes to go back with Dante to Miami. Make sure that they have weapons as well. Also, call and have my personal jet gassed and ready for Dante."

"Yes, sir!" Carlos replied before leaving the office just as Carmen and Natalie entered.

"Dante, is it true you are leaving us?" Carmen asked, as she stopped beside him.

"Only for a little while," Dante answered, as Natalie wrapped herself around him and leaned into his side. "I should be back within two weeks. But if either of you need me, I'll return here no questions asked."

Smiling at his response, Carmen leaned into Dante. She gave him a hug and a kiss on the cheek. After releasing him, she added, "You just make sure that you make it back to us safely, okay?"

After finishing up with Dominic, Natalie left the office with him. He headed towards the front door, where he saw James and Carlos talking with one another.

"Everything is ready!" Carlos told Dante and explained further, "The limo will take you to the jet and from there you will be on your way. Have a safe trip there and try not to stay away too long."

Smiling as he dapped up with Carlos, Dante turned to James and asked, "What's up, J? You ready?"

"I move when you move, bro!" James replied with a smile.

Turning back and looking towards the hallway, Dante saw Carmen walking towards him with a large brown envelope, which she handed to him.

"This is for you from both Dominic and me. If you need more, just let us know and we will have it sent to you," Carmen explained to Dante.

Accepting the envelope he felt was filled with money, Dante kissed Carmen's cheek and said, "Thank you, Carmen."

"You just be careful!" Carmen warned. She then quickly turned and walked off before Dante could see her crying.

Turning back towards the door, Dante handed both his bags and the envelope to James and told him to wait for him outside in the limo.

As she began to tear up, Dante wiped her face and said, "Come on, beautiful! No reason why you should be crying. I'll be back."

"I'm just going to miss you," she told him, reaching up and wrapping her arms tightly around his neck. "I love you, Dante."

"I love you, too, Natalie. You have both my and Vanessa's numbers if you want to get in contact with me," Dante told her as they broke apart. He wiped her face again, winking his eye at her, making her smile.

Accepting the kiss that Dante gave her, Natalie stepped to the front door and stood watching as he walked off toward the limo. He stopped and spoke with Gomez briefly, smiling and shaking hands with him.

Waving when Dante looked back up at her, Natalie smiled as Dante gave a goodbye wink. Then he climbed inside the limo as the driver closed the door behind him.

15

Receiving his call a few hours ago telling her what time to pick
him up, Vanessa excitedly pulled up onto the airstrip where she
was supposed to meet, where she found a car and two SUVs
already parked out on the strip.

She wondered if she was at the right place when she saw the
blinking lights and heard the plane. Vanessa turned her attention to
the white and dark blue jet that was landing.

She shifted her eyes to the Mercedes Benz and a white-suited
gentleman climbing out. She turned her attention back to the jet,
just as the hatch door was opening and the steps were let down.

Vanessa saw ten or eleven men step off the jet, followed by a
white man in a dark grey cotton sweat suit carrying bags in his
hand. Vanessa broke out in a huge smile and rushed over from her
truck as soon as she saw Dante walking off the jet last.

"Dante!"

Dante heard his name being called. He looked to the far right
as his security team pulled their weapons and pointed. He yelled at
his team to stand down after realizing it was Vanessa.

"Relax, fellas!" Dante yelled out, as he stepped through the
team of armed security guards and walked towards Vanessa with a
smile.

"Damn, nigga!" Vanessa said, as she threw her arms around his
neck, hugging him tightly.

"What's up, Vanessa?" Dante said, releasing her. "You looking
good, lil sis!"

"Look at you, nigga!" Vanessa told him, smiling at seeing Dante was bigger than before he left. "You done put on some more weight and muscle, I see."

"Just a lil something!" Dante replied still smiling.

"And what's up with all these niggas you got with you? Who they?" she asked, just as she and Dante heard his named being called out.

Looking over his shoulder, he saw James waving him over to a middle-aged, white gentleman in a suit. Dante looked back to Vanessa as she asked, "Who's the white guy you brought back with you?"

"Come on! I'll introduce you," Dante told Vanessa, leading her over to where James was standing with the other man.

"Yo, Dante! Guy here says he needs to talk with you," James told Dante, while staring over at Vanessa.

"Who you?" Dante asked the guy, noticing the way his team surrounded the unknown man.

"G-Good morning, Mr. Black-Blackwell, sir!" the white man began nervously. He took a quick breath and continued, "My name is Greg Wilson and I was assigned to you by a Mr. Dominic Saldana to take care of matters that you may need assistance with."

"What can you do for me that I can't do for myself?" Dante asked, as he stood staring hard at the guy.

"It's not a matter of what I can do that you cannot, Mr. Blackwell. It's a matter of my being able to handle things fast and when you need them, just as I've brought you vehicles for you and your men," he told Dante, waving his open hand back at the Mercedes and the two Yukons.

Nodding his head slowly, Dante shifted his eyes back to Greg Wilson before calling to James, "Get Greg's contact number so we'll be able to reach him."

Turning back to Vanessa and noticing the timid smile and expression on her face, he asked, "What's wrong, Nessa?"

Shaking her head, Vanessa looked to the right of Dante as James stepped up beside him.

"Dante, Wilson says Dominic already paid for us to stay at some penthouse out on Miami Beach," James informed.

"Alright!" Dante replied before smirking at the way James was checking out Vanessa. "James, meet my brother's wife, Vanessa."

"How you doing, Vanessa?" James said, shaking her hand.

"What's up, James?" Vanessa replied, smirking as she too noticed the way he was looking at her.

"J, go ahead and let Wilson take you to the penthouse and take the team with you," Dante told James. "I'ma roll with my sister."

"I got you, but hit me up if you need me, bro!" James told Dante, touching fists with him. Then he said goodbye to Vanessa, whose smile provided an acknowledged goodbye.

Handing his bags off to one of the men on his security team, Dante turned back to Vanessa and said, "So, what's up? You ready to go?"

* * *

"So, what's up, Vanessa?" Dante asked, after he and Vanessa left the airstrip.

"What are you talking about?" Vanessa asked, glancing over at Dante again.

"Look!" Dante started, as he pulled a box of Black & Mild's from his pocket, "I know I been gone a lil minute now but I'm still the same Dante."

"Why you say that?"

"Because I peeped how you keep staring at me smiling. What's really up with that?"

Quiet for a moment, Vanessa glanced over at Dante and said, "You just seem a little different from how you used to be before you left."

"How?"

"You just seem different," she repeated. She added, "First, you never used to smile so much but now you're constantly smiling and seem happy. You seem relaxed and I noticed you got that whole thinking thing still but you're quicker at using it than before you left."

Hearing Vanessa's words and considering what she just told him, Dante changed the subject asking, "So, where we going?"

"To see Angela and your daughter," Vanessa answered, cutting her eyes over to Dante, noticing how he had changed the topic from himself.

"So, who all know I'm back?"

"Nobody! You told me not to tell anyone, right?"

"And you actually listened?"

Vanessa smiled and playfully punched Dante in the arm, which he grabbed and laughed. She said, "We can go to the house after we leave from seeing Angela and Mya."

"Naw! I'm good, Vanessa!"

"Relax, Dante! Alinna's not there anyway. She mostly stays with that dude she been seeing."

Looking over at Vanessa before shaking his head and turning his attention out the window, Dante asked, "What's up? Have y'all heard anything else from this clown, Fish Man?"

"No!" Vanessa replied. "But Wesley is looking into finding out what he can about his ass, though."

"I also wanna talk to Wesley."

"He supposed to call me later on," she told him and asked, "What's up with the white boy? James?"

"Why?" Dante asked, smirking as he looked back over at Vanessa.

"Dante, don't play with me, boy. The white boy cute and all but he not my type and Andre would kill that white boy for real."

"I don't know about that," Dante said, still smirking as Vanessa shot him a look.

"What you trying to say, Dante?" Vanessa asked him. "Who's this white boy?"

"Let's just say that I've seen James get down and that white boy about his issue, Nessa. Believe me!"

Deciding to leave the topic alone, Vanessa continued driving to get breakfast and gas, which Dante paid for.

Pulling up in front of Angela's house ten minutes later, Vanessa shut off the BMW and climbed out of the car. As they walked around the front of the car, Dante asked about his nephew A.J.

"He with Andre getting a haircut today. We'll see him later," Vanessa replied, as they walked up the walkway to the front door.

Dante knocked on the front door and turned around to look over the neighborhood. Vanessa noticed that he still had his old ways about him.

He turned around just as the front door opened and Angela stepped into the doorway. Vanessa stepped to the side as she watched Angela's eyes shift directly to Dante.

"What's up, Angela?" Dante spoke as Angela's hands shot up and covered her mouth, tears in her eyes.

"Oh my God, Dante!" Angela cried, just before she rushed toward him.

Catching Angela as she threw herself at him, Dante held her a few moments while she hugged him and cried.

"Oh God, Dante!" Angela said, as she released him and stepped back. She looked him over. "You look really good! You've gained weight and some more muscle."

"I told you!" Vanessa agreed, as she walked past both Dante and Angela and into the house.

Shaking his head with a smile on his face, Dante looked back at Angela, catching her staring at him.

"You look a little different," she told him. "Older and calmer."

"I'm still me!" Dante replied before asking, "Where's Mya?"

"She's inside with her brother watching cartoons," Angela replied, grabbing Dante's hand and leading him into the house. "Wait until you see how big the both of them are now, Dante."

Dante followed Angela to the den where Vanessa had given something to eat to the kids. He stood there staring at both of them and realized they were now old enough to feed themselves.

Vanessa said something to Mya and D.J, as they turned around and looked in Dante's direction. Both children broke out in a big smile.

"Daddy!" Mya and D.J. cried together.

Dante walked over to his kids, as both of them climbed to their feet and reached up to him. He picked up both kids just as Vanessa said, "They both know who you are, Dante. We make sure that they see your pictures I got and we talk about you to them all the time."

Looking back to his kids, while directly particular attention to his son, Dante stood smiling and listening to the boy as he struggled to communicate. Mya simply held on to his neck and hugged him.

* * *

Dante spent some time with his daughter and son, enjoying breakfast with both of them. He noticed how protective D.J. was over his older sister, as well as the affection Mya displayed by the need to hold her younger brother's hand or always sit next to him. Dante smiled at these things, continuing to enjoy their company.

"Dante!"

Dante looked over his left shoulder upon hearing his name and saw Angela motioning him over. Vanessa walked back into the den with the children. Dante stood up from the sofa picking up the kids dishes before he followed Angela into the dining room. On the table sat a navy blue folder.

"What's that?" Dante asked, as Angela took the plates from him.

"It's the information you asked for about Alex Whitehead," Angela explained, as she walked off and headed into the kitchen.

Dante sat down in one of the chairs and opened the folder. He began reading through the information that was inside the file about Agent Alex Whitehead.

"Why isn't there a picture of this guy in here?" Dante asked, looking up and to his right as Angela stepped up beside him.

"He's undercover, Dante! DEA won't let out a picture of him because of that."

"So, who are Agent Monica Martin and Agent Paul Young?"

"The information I got back says that Monica Martin is actually Alex Whitehead's partner and Paul Young is supposedly their back-up. Monica Martin has been with the DEA for ten years, and has been Alex's partner for eight of those years."

Nodding his head in acknowledgment of what was just explained to him, Dante focused back on reading the file when his cell phone rang.

"Yeah!" Dante answered after digging out his phone.

"Hey baby! You made it to Miami yet?"

Smiling at hearing Natalie's voice, Dante stood up from the table, walked into the living room, and said, "What's up, beautiful? Yeah! I just got to Miami a few minutes ago. I'm with Vanessa and the kids now."

"I miss you."

"Really?"

"Dante, stop playing! You know I miss you."

"Yeah, I know. I miss you too, Natalie."

"I'll let you finish spending time with your sister and the kids. Tell Vanessa I said hi...and I love you, Dante."

Dante hung up the phone after telling Natalie he loved her back. Then he headed back into the dining room, noticing the way in which Angela was watching him.

"So, that was her, huh?" Angela asked, as Dante stopped next to her at the table. "That was Natalie."

Dante didn't even bother asking how she knew her name. He figured Vanessa had told her. He answered, "Yeah! That was her!"

"I can tell," Angela replied. "I saw the smile on your face when you answered your phone. I've never seen you smile like that before."

Changing the topic, Dante asked, "So, is this all the information you've got on Alex Whitehead and the other two agents working with him?"

"It's all the DEA sent over."

"So, basically we're looking for a ghost then, huh?"

"Dante!" Vanessa called, as she walked into the dining room.

"What's up?" he asked, turning to face her, noticing a strange look on her face.

"Dante, we gotta go! Amber just got into some shit with some Haitians."

"Haitians?"

"That's what she said. We gotta go!"

Dante told Angela he would give her a call later and that he'd return the folder when he was finished with it. He then stopped to say goodbye to D.J. and Mya, and explain that he would be back soon. He then rushed back out to Vanessa's truck, where he found her already behind the wheel talking on the phone.

Climbing inside the truck and hearing Vanessa say Alinna's name as he was closing the passenger door, Dante dug out his ringing phone and answered, "Yeah!"

"This is James! Everything's good at the penthouse, bro! You gotta see this . . ."

"J, listen!" Dante interrupted. "I gotta meet with some of my family. Shit just jumped off and I wanna find out what's up."

"Where am I meeting you at?"

"Naw, you . . ."

"Don't even say it!" James cut in before Dante could finish. "I came down here to help, not chill up in some penthouse. Where am I meeting you at?"

"Hold on!" Dante told James, looking over at Vanessa to see if she was off the phone. "Vanessa, where we headed?"

"Card City!" she answered.

Relaying the information to James, he said that he would use the GPS in the Benz. Getting the address from Vanessa, he handed it off to James.

"Dante, look!" Vanessa said as soon as she saw that Dante hung up the phone. "I'ma tell you now before we get there. Alinna is gonna be there. So don't trip when you see her."

"This not about Alinna, Vanessa. I'm here because you called me and said the family needed help. Period!"

Nodding her head in agreement, Vanessa cut her eyes over to Dante to see if he really meant it, before focusing back on the road wondering if Dante was really over Alinna.

* * *

Alinna pulled up to Amber's spot and saw Wesley, Tony T, Amber, and Harmony all talking in front of the trap house. She parked her BMW in front of Tony T's Aston Martin and turned to Alex to ask him to stay in the car moments too late as he was already climbing out.

Shaking her head while climbing out of the car, Alinna slammed the door shut and walked around to the front of the BMW, where Alex was waiting telling him, "I wish you would have stayed inside the car, Alex."

"You said your friend had a problem, so we're here to find out what. Come on!" Alex told her, as he gently pushed her forward in the front yard. He was sure it was one of the many trap houses where Alinna and her friends sold drugs.

"What the fuck he doing here?" Tony T asked, as soon as Alinna and Alex walked in.

"He's with me," Alinna answered, shooting Tony T a look. Then she rolled her eyes, looked over to Amber, and asked, "What happened, Amber?"

"Here come Dre now!" Harmony announced, nodding out to Dre's Land Rover as it pulled up.

Looking from the Land Rover to Alex, Alinna grabbed his hand. She wanted to tell him to go get back inside the car, but she didn't want to embarrass him in front of everyone.

"What the fuck his ass doing here?" Dre asked, as he walked up and stared at Alex.

"Don't worry about it!" Alinna spoke up. "He with me and I'm sure you're here to find out what's happening with Amber. Try focusing on that and not on Alex."

"Dre chill!" Tony T followed, seeing the look on his boy's face.

"Anyways!" Harmony said loudly to draw attention to her. "Can we get to what's important, please?"

"What happened, Amber?" Alinna asked again, as she watched Amber and Wesley talking with each other.

Turning her attention back to the others, Amber began to explain what had happened, from the time she noticed she was being followed until when she was cut off by an Expedition and blocked from getting to her next drop-off. She then smashed into another Expedition when she threw her Acura in reverse after seeing men armed with guns jump out of the vehicle in front of her.

"How do you know they was Haitians?" Alex asked.

"Dude, shut the fuck up!" Dre told him, mean-mugging Alex.

"Naw! That's a good question," Alinna said, cutting her eyes to Dre before looking back at Amber and asking, "Are you sure they was Haitians, Amber?"

"What the blood clot?" Wesley spoke up for the first time, pulling out his burner and staring out at the streets as two Yukons and a Benz pulled up in front of the spot.

"Who the fuck is that?" Tony T said, as he pulled out his banger, staring at the rides.

"Hold up! Isn't that Vanessa's truck pulling up, too?" Harmony asked, noticing the BMW truck parking next to Dre's Land Rover.

Seeing a white man climb out of the smoke-gray Benz, followed by armed men jumping out of both Yukons, Alinna heard Harmony scream just as she took off past her, rushing towards the front of the trap house.

"Blood clot!" Wesley said, smiling now at seeing who climbed out of the front seat of Vanessa's truck.

"Oh shit!" Both Dre and Tony T said together, with Dre adding, "My muthafucking nigga home!"

Alinna watched as Dante stepped from Vanessa's truck as Harmony ran up and hugged him. She heard Alex ask who Dante was.

"Dis me brethren! The bad boy rasta man come home!" Wesley said happily, as Dante, Harmony, Vanessa, and James walked up.

"My muthafucking brother!" Dre said, as he and Dante embraced each other.

Releasing Dre and then embracing Tony T and Amber, Dante turned around to see a huge smiling Wesley. In patois, he said, "What's up, Wesley? You been handling what I told you?"

"She right behind you, me brethren, only that she mess with the blood clot boy there with her," Wesley answered in patois.

Nodding his head, Dante turned back to a smiling Amber and said in English, "What's up, cutie? You alright?"

Nodding her head yes and smiling at Dante, Amber said, "What happen to you? You done went away and came back even sexier then when you left."

Smirking at Amber while giving her a wink Dante answered, "Let's all go inside and talk. Try to figure this shit out."

"What's up with all them?" Dre asked, nodding back out to all the suit-wearing men in the middle of the street.

"James!" Dante called out.

"What's up, bro?" he answered.

"Tell the team to relax and come join us inside the house," Dante told James. He shifted his eyes over to Alinna's friend and said, "Whoever you is, wait for Alinna out in her ride."

"Hold up!" Alinna spoke up. "First of all, you don't come back here demanding shit. Alex is with me."

Ignoring Alinna as he stared at her friend, Dante calmly said, "I don't know you which means I don't trust you either so you can either wait in the car or you can wait in the trunk for Alinna. Decide now!"

Dante stared at the new guy a moment before noticing the way Alinna was looking at him. Alex called to Alinna, but she only replied, "Go wait in the car, Alex."

Smiling as Tony T nudged him in the side laughing, Dre watched the bitch-ass nigga walk out to Alinna's car. He looked back at Dante and said, "Damn, it's good as fuck to have your ass back home, fam."

16

Once everyone was packed inside the trap house, Dante
introduced them to James.

After the introductions were complete, Dante held up his hand
to stop the questions that started. Then he turned to Amber and
asked her to tell him what had happened between her and the
Haitians had shot at her.

Dante listened as Amber broke down the full story of what had
happened. He even asked her to repeat a few things. He wanted to
make sure it all added up. Then he held up his hand to stop Amber
from going any further.

"Wait a minute! You said you smashed into one of the SUVs?
The one behind you, right?" Dante asked her, as he stared at
Amber, his face balled up as he played out everything in his head.

Nodding her head yes, Amber said, "I was trying to get the hell
outta there."

"And they just let you go?" James asked, drawing everyone's
attention.

"You peeped what I'm thinking, J!" Dante asked James, as he
looked over at Amber and back to James.

"I think so," James answered, as he folded his arms across his
chest.

"Well, how about the two of you fill us in if you got it figured
out already!" Alinna demanded, staring straight at Dante.

Dante ignored the attention Alinna was looking for, along with
the attitude she was throwing his way. He replied, "I figure that if

they really wanted Amber dead, that was the perfect chance right there."

"They only wanted to scare her and send a message," James added, catching Dante nodding his head in agreement.

"What type of message are the Haitians trying to send us?" Harmony asked. "We ain't got problems with them."

"True!" Dante agreed. Then he said, "We do have problems with this clown, Fish Man, though."

"So, what you saying, fam?" Dre asked from across the room, with both thick arms folded across his chest.

"I can't say for sure yet but what it looks like is that this nigga, Fish Man, done went and teamed up with these Haitians to get at us," Dante explained as he sat looking around the room at the others.

"Ain't this some shit!" Tony T said, as he leaned back in his seat next to Harmony on the brown, worn-out couch.

"So, what's the plan?" Alinna asked, still staring at Dante.

Dante heard the question and noticed the way everyone was waiting and staring at him for a reply. After a few moments he said, "Alright! I know how each of y'all handle business but until we figure this shit out, I'm placing security on all three of the girls. Alinna, I'm giving you two guards since you is who this nigga, Fish Man, got the beef with. And also, I think it's time y'all moved out of the house. If Fish Man really playing the game like this, I'm sure he knows where each of you lays your heads at."

"Wait a minute . . ."

"Alinna, can you just stop talking for a minute and listen to what the hell is being said," Dante told her, seeing the expression on her face.

"Dante!" James said, drawing his attention over to him. "Since you're putting security on all the girls and want them to move out of their house, why not have everyone just move into the penthouse where we're at? Dominic bought out the whole top two floors and from what I've seen, it's more than enough space for all of us."

"Who the hell is Dominic and what penthouse does Dante have?" Alinna asked, staring at James and then over to Dante.

"Listen good Alinna because I won't repeat myself again," Dante told her. "You either want my help or you don't. As for everybody else, I'ma do whatever must be done to make sure they straight. You got the choice to accept my help and everything I'm offering or you can take your chances on your own. I don't really give a fuck either way."

Staring at Dante in shock and feeling a bit hurt after hearing how he spoke to her in front of everybody, Alinna kept her eyes on him as he stood up and started for the front door. Everyone else followed.

"You alright?" Vanessa asked, walking beside Alinna.

Looking from the door after everybody followed Dante, Alinna met Vanessa's eyes and said, "What was that just now?"

"Come on, Alinna!" Vanessa said in a soft tone of voice. "You can't tell me you don't see the change in Dante. He not the same as before he left and he may or may not still have feelings for you. But after what happened between the two of you, do you really think he's gonna respond to you how he once did?"

"Why didn't you tell me he was back, Vanessa?"

"He told me not to say anything."

"Vanessa!" Amber interrupted, as she stepped back into the house.

"Yeah! What's up, Amber?" Vanessa said, looking from Alinna to Amber at the front door.

"Dante wants you and Alinna to come out here," Amber told them. Seeing the look on Alinna's face, she asked, "Alinna, you okay, girl?"

"I'm fine," Alinna answered, as she walked off brushing past Amber as she stepped out the front door.

"What's wrong with her?" Amber asked, looking back at Vanessa.

"She good!" Vanessa replied, as she walked over to the front door. "Come on! Let's see what Dante wants."

Once Vanessa finally showed up outside with Amber and the others, Dante assigned one of the armed guards to Vanessa. After introducing the two, he made sure the guard knew that if anything happened to Vanessa, he would be better off killing himself.

"Vanessa, do me a favor," Dante asked, as he nodded over toward Alinna and the guy she was talking to. "Let your girl know I've got other things to do and if she wants my help, then she need to bring her ass over here."

"Amber, let me talk to Dante really fast, please!" Vanessa asked her girl. She then held up her hand toward her new guard, as she pulled Dante off to the side and asked, "Dante, what's up?"

"What you mean?"

"I mean this attitude and the way you treating Alinna. You do remember that's your son's mother, right?

"Vanessa, I'm done playing with Alinna. I've tried to do everything I could. Look! I'ma do everything I can to deal with this problem with Fish Man and the Haitians but after that I'm done. I'm out of here. Period!"

"So you not staying? You going back to Arizona?"

"Pretty much."

"What about Mya and D.J.?"

"I want them to stay with their moms, but I will come back to see them."

"Truthfully, Dante. I think you're running because you still have feelings for Alinna and you're jealous of Alex."

"Jealous of Alex! Hold on!" Dante said, as he shifted his eyes over to where Alinna and her supposedly new guy were talking near her BMW.

"Dante, what's up?" Vanessa asked, noticing the change in Dante's facial expression. "What's the matter?"

Ignoring her question, Dante walked away from the group and pulled his burner out as he stepped up beside Alinna, facing her man.

"Dante, what the fuck are you doing?" Alinna asked, noticing the gun.

Ignoring Alinna while staring straight at Alex, Dante calmly asked, "What's your name, dude?"

"Dante, what the hell . . . !"

"Alinna, come on!" James interrupted, as he walked up and reached out to escort her away.

"Get the fuck off me!" Alinna yelled, pushing James in the chest. She then turned back to Dante, standing between him and Alex.

"Get her outta here!" Dante demanded, still staring straight at Alex.

"Muthafucker! Don't touch me!" Alinna yelled, as James snatched her up and walked away with her across his shoulders.

Fam, what's up?" Dre asked, as he, Tony T, Vanessa, and Wesley walked up. "What the play is, bruh?"

"Who is this nigga?" Dante asked, never taking his eyes off of him. "Where he come from? Who checked him out?"

"What you mean, Dante?" Vanessa asked, pushing Dre out of the way so that she could stand next to Dante. "This the same guy I told you about. This Alinna's new man."

"What's your name, homeboy?" Dante asked, addressing the question to Alinna's man.

"Man, what's this . . . ,"

Suddenly, Alex was cut off as Dante's hand shot up. He was now staring down the front of a .45.

Ignoring Alinna's yells from behind him, Dante held homeboy's eyes as he calmly asked again, "What's your name, dude?"

"Alex!"

"Alex what?"

"Williams! It's Alex Williams!"

"Williams, huh?" Dante repeated, slowly smirking while still holding Alex's eyes. He slowly lowered the burner and said, "My fault, playboy. I thought you was somebody else."

Dante turned and started back over towards the Benz when someone grabbed his arm. Looking back, he saw Vanessa's hard staring eyes. She asked, "What the fuck was that, Dante? That's not like you. What are you up to?"

Shifting his eyes from Vanessa back over to Alex, he saw Alinna walk back up to her man. Dante ignored the others who were now crowding around him with questioning looks on their faces.

"Bro, what's up?" James asked, staring from Dante over to Alinna and the guy Dante was now staring back at.

"Yo, Whitehead!" Dante called out, watching as Alex looked his way. "We cool, right?"

"Yeah!" Alex answered. "We cool, man!"

Nodding his head, Dante turned his attention back to the others just as Vanessa spoke up, "Are you planning on telling us what the fuck is going on, Dante? Why the hell you so worried about Alex for?"

"How long y'all know this dude, Alex?" Dante asked, looking around at each of their faces.

"I really don't fuck with the guy!" Dre spoke up.

"Dante, Alex been messing with Alinna ever since you and her broke up," Vanessa explained in a calmer voice.

"Harmony!" Dante said, looking from Vanessa over to where Alinna was still talking to the new man she was fucking. "I'ma need you to handle something for me, baby girl."

"What you need, bro?" Harmony asked, smiling at Dante.

"Give Amber the keys to your ride and go with Alinna and Alex. I'ma need you to get Alinna away from homeboy for me, alright?"

"I got you, boo."

"Dante, what's going on?" Vanessa asked, as Harmony handed Amber her keys starting in Alinna and Alex's direction.

Looking from Harmony to Vanessa, Dante said, "I'ma tell y'all this. The next time y'all decide to allow someone outside into the family, make sure one of y'all check that person out first."

"What ya mean, rude boy?" Wesley asked, folding his arms across his chest as he held his eyes locked on Dante.

"Tell me something!" Dante asked, looking around at the rest of the crew. "What was homeboy's name again?"

"You mean Alinna's dude, right?" Tony T asked.

"Yeah!" Dante answered. "What's dude's name?"

"He says it's Alex Williams," James spoke up, staring at Dante.

"He say, huh," Dante repeated. "Listen y'all! If any of you was listening when I called homeboy's name just now, he answered to . . . ?"

"Whitehead!" Amber announced, drawing the others attention to her.

Nodding his head and smiling at Amber, Dante winked at her and said, "If y'all remember the captain that got killed back when Angela was still a lieutenant, his name was Ben Whitehead. Same last name as our friend, Alex, over there with Alinna and Harmony."

"Hold up!" Amber said, putting her hand up for Dante to stop talking for a few moment. "So, what you saying is that Alex is this dead captain's son, Dante?"

"Pretty much!" Dante answered, slowly nodding his head. "Homeboy undercover with the D.E.A. I'm pretty sure he's been watching you since he been fucking with Alinna."

"How the hell you know all this?" Vanessa asked, before answering her own question. "That's what Angela wanted to tell you, isn't it? That's the stuff you been reading in that file inside the truck, isn't it?"

Nodding his head, Dante continued, "Look! I want y'all to start closing down each of the spots y'all running and we moving out of the house today. Everyone's moving into the penthouse until we find a new spot to rest our heads."

"What we doing about the blood clot boy over there?" Wesley asked, nodding over toward Alex, Alinna, and Harmony.

"Don't worry about him!" Dante told Wesley, looking over to see him climbing inside the BMW. "I'ma handle homeboy real soon."

17

Alex was unable to focus on anything that Alinna and Har-mony were saying as he sat staring out the window thinking about the encounter with the man who had murdered his father. He snapped out of his deep thought only when he heard Alinna yell his name.

"Yeah!" Alex answered, turning and looking back over to her, meeting her concerned eyes.

"Baby, you okay?"

"Yeah, I'm just thinking."

"Don't waste your time thinking about Dante."

"So, that's your son's father, huh?"

Sighing deeply, Alinna answered, "Yeah! That's his crazy ass!"

"Where he been at?" Alex asked. "He just popped up out of nowhere."

"He been . . ."

"That's just how Dante is," Harmony spoke up, cutting off Alinna. "Dante just moves like that. You'll get used to it."

"I hope not!" Alex replied as his cell phone vibrated inside his pocket. Pulling out the phone, he saw that he received a text message.

"Who's that?" Alinna asked, seeing Alex looking at his cell phone.

"Text message!" Alex answered, sliding the phone back into his pocket. "Monica asking where I was."

Staring at Alex a moment, Alinna slowly nodded her head and focused back on the road without saying anything.

Once Alinna made it to his condo, Alex leaned over and kissed Alinna goodbye. As he was climbing out of her car, she called his name.

"Yeah!" Alex responded, ducking his head back inside the car.

"Alex, you sure you okay?"

"Yeah! I'm good, Alinna." Alex answered with a smile. "I'ma call you later, alright?"

"Alright."

Alex closed the car door and started walking towards his condo. When Alex got to his front door, he turned around and watched Alinna drive off.

Pulling out his cell phone, Alex pulled up Monica's number and was just about to call her when he looked and saw a car pulling up.

"Son of a bitch!" Alex cursed, recognizing the Mercedes that pulled to a stop in front of his condo.

Sliding the cell phone back into his pocket, Alex walked back out to the edge of the walkway as Dante climbed from behind the driver's seat of the Benz.

"What are you doing here?" Alex asked, staring at Dante, as he calmly shut the car door and walked around to the front of the Benz, leaning back onto the hood.

"So, Alex!" Dante started, fold his arms across his chest. "I think we should talk."

"Talk about what?"

"How about we start with Alinna?"

"Dante, look! I know you two . . ."

Naw!" Dante cut in. "I'm sure you know me and Alinna was together. What I mean by talking about Alinna is how much information you have on her."

"W-What?"

"Come on, Alex! I'm sure you know by now that I know you're D.E.A. and who your father was. Why don't you make this easy and tell me what you got on Alinna."

Staring straight into the eyes of the man who murdered his father, Alex felt his anger building. "You know what, you son of a bitch? You're right! I am D.E.A. and I've got enough information on Alinna's stupid ass, as well as the rest of her little crew, to lock them up for the rest of their lives. But I'll make a deal with you. Turn yourself in and admit to my father's murder and I'll leave your little girlfriend and her crew alone."

Continuing to stare back at the D.E.A. agent, Dante slowly began to smile. His smile then turned into a light laugh, as he pushed himself off the front of the Benz.

"Freeze, mutha . . . ," Alex started, reaching for the weapon he had inside his holster. Out of nowhere, his right arm was tightly wrapped around his neck with his other arm folded behind his back, pushed up towards his shoulder blades, which caused him to yell out in pain.

James held the guy in a tight chokehold after creeping up on him from behind, while the agent wasn't fully paying attention. Dante said, "Seems like you won't be sticking around long enough to turn shit in for a life sentence to be given to nobody, Agent Alex Whitehead."

* * *

Alinna had strong feelings about moving into a penthouse that belonged to Dante. Still, she carried a bag she packed while the security detail carried four more bags behind her.

"Alinna, you alright, girl?" Harmony asked, as the two of them took the elevator together to the penthouse floor, where the others were waiting.

"I'm just not feeling this moving in here with Dante's ass," Alinna explained. "I would rather stay back at the house."

"Alinna, can I be honest with you?"

"What's up, girl?"

"You don't know it but Dante still loves you."

"He told you that?" Alinna asked, looking over to Harmony.

Nodding her head, Harmony answered, "Back after I got shot and before Dante left, we had a long talk about you, and he admitted that he fucked up for hurting you. He said that it was killing him more because your trust meant a lot to him. I don't know if you've noticed it or not. I think after you ended things with him and he moved away, it now looks as if his love for you may now be something else."

"What you mean something else?"

"I mean, it looks like Dante may hate you a little now. And with how you're acting with him, it's not making things between the two of you any better."

Stepping off the elevator as it opened on the penthouse floor, four of Dante's security guards stared directly at the two women. Alinna ignored their stares as she replayed what Harmony had just told her.

"Thank you!" Alinna and Harmony said to the guard who opened the door for them.

"Alinna, you okay?" Harmony asked, as she followed her girl inside the penthouse.

"Yeah!" Alinna lied.

Vanessa called out to her walking out from the kitchen, with Dre following right behind her.

"Girl, look at this place!" Harmony said, smiling as she looked around. Both Vanessa and Dre stopped in front of her

"Dante not with y'all?" Vanessa asked.

"Why would he be with us, Vanessa?" Alinna asked with an attitude. The she dropped her bag beside the sofa she was standing next to.

"Mrs. Blackwell, your bags, ma'am," one of Alinna's guards announced, as he and his partner entered the penthouse.

Sucking her teeth, Alinna turned back to a smiling Vanessa and Harmony. "Where the hell is Dante's ass, anyway?"

"He just called," Amber announced, as she walked into the room. "He and James say they'll be here in a little while."

"Where's D.J.?" Alinna then asked, walking passed Vanessa and ignoring the way that Dre was looking at her.

"Rose has both D.J. and A.J.," Vanessa told her. "They're in the back watching television."

Watching Alinna as she looked around the penthouse, Vanessa shook her head. She looked over at the way her man was looking at Alinna asking, "Andre, what's wrong with you?"

"Nothing!" Dre answered, as he walked off and headed toward the sliding-glass door that led out onto the balcony.

Following Dre outside, Vanessa watched him pull out a box of Newport's. She closed the door and turned and faced Andre asking, "What was that just now? Why was you just staring at Alinna like that?"

Cutting his eyes over to Vanessa, Dre shook his head and said, "I'm really tired of how she keeps treating my brother. My nigga just keeps going out his way for this bitch and she just keeps popping off attitude and talking shit. I'm surprised Dante ain't snap on her ass yet."

"Andre, that's between Alinna and Dante. Why are you so upset?"

"Because I don't like to see my nigga the way he is," Dre answered. "Dante don't show too much of his self for a reason. We not blood brothers but I'm the only family he's got. His mother left him by his self-inside the house she was about to lose right after this father was killed. Dante used to live on the streets for a long time until my mom took him in after he helped me handle six guys that tried to jump me. He may have fucked up, but what the rest of y'all fail to understand is that my boy did what he did for Alinna's ass and she too stupid to see it."

"Andre, I didn't know all that."

"Nobody knows what I just told you."

Hearing the sliding glass door opening behind them, both Dre and Vanessa looked back as Dante was stepping out onto the balcony with them.

"What's up, family? Y'all hungry?" Dante asked, nodding to Dre as Vanessa walked over and gave him a hug around the waist.

"Hell, yeah. We wanna eat!" Dre said, smiling as he pushed away from the rail to face Dante and Vanessa. He tossed the butt from his cigarette over his shoulder and off the balcony rail. "What you bought to eat?"

"Do it really even matter, Andrew?" Vanessa asked, shooting him a look.

"Women, what you trying to say?" Dre asked Vanessa, seeing her slowly smiling at him.

"Go check!" Dante told Dre, as he stepped out onto the balcony with Vanessa. When he saw the look on her face, he reached up and gently brushed the back of his hand down the side of her face and asked, "Baby sis, you alright?"

"I'm good, Dante," Vanessa answered, as she wrapped her arms around his waist, leaned in, and said, "You know I really love you, right?"

"I love you, too, Vanessa," Dante replied, as he wrapped his arms around her.

"Am I interrupting something?"

Hearing and recognizing Alinna's voice, Dante and Vanessa looked back at the sliding-glass door to see Alinna standing there with her arms folded across her chest. Her face was balled up as she stared at them.

Shaking his head, Dante kissed Vanessa on the forehead and then whispered into her ear, saying that he would talk to her later.

Alinna watched Dante as he walked back inside, completely ignoring her. Then she walked over to Vanessa and asked, "What the hell was just going on, Vanessa?"

"None of your business!" Vanessa answered, with just as much attitude. She went to go inside when Alinna grabbed her arm, stopping her short.

Snapping Vanessa around to face her, Alinna said, "Do not play with me. What was that between you and Dante just now?"

"Oh, so you jealous now?" Vanessa said, slowly smiling at Alinna. "Well, don't worry. Dante isn't my type. I love him like a brother. Just so you know, though. The woman you should be worried about is the one he left back in Arizona to come here and help us."

"What the hell are you talking about, Vanessa?"

"Oh, that's right! You don't know about Dante's new woman, do you? Well maybe if you had been paying attention, you would have noticed that Dante has a woman now. Just pay attention how he acts with you now."

Alinna stared at Vanessa as she walked back into the penthouse. She found herself playing back in her head what Vanessa told her about Dante and some other bitch back in another state.

* * *

"What in the hell!" Agent Monica Martin said in disbelief and shock, as she and Agent Paul Young pulled up in front of the crowd that had surrounded the front of her partner's condo.

"What the hell is all this?" Agent Young asked, climbing from the car as soon as Agent Martin stopped.

Jumping out right behind him, Agent Martin slammed the car door and headed towards the front door to the condo, ignoring the stares and pointing from the crowd and media.

After showing their identification, they were introduced to the detective in charge. Both agents then flashed their badges to the lead detective.

"What the hell is D.E.A. doing here?" Detective Howard Fuller inquired, after seeing the two agents I.D.s.

"What's happened here?" Agent Martin asked, ignoring the detective's questions. "Where's my partner?"

"Whoa!" Detective Fuller said, raising up his hands for the agent to hold on. "What do you mean your partner?"

"What the fuck is going on upstairs?" Agent Martin interrupted, seeing the trail of EM techs and fire department personnel going up and down the stairs.

Not even waiting for an answer, Agent Martin took off, rushing up the stairs two at a time.

Once upstairs, she pushed her way through the crowded hallway, flashing her I.D. to two officers who tried to stop and question her. Agent Martin snapped away from them and continued on towards the bedroom where everyone was in a flurry.

Stopping right inside the bedroom doorway, Agent Martin stood staring at the body that was on top of the bed, covered with a white sheet. She was able to see the shape of the body print.

Walking over to the bedside, she reached over, grabbed the sheet, and pulled it back uncovering the body. It was then that she discovered what she knew was already true. She cried out, "Oh God, no!"

"Agent Martin," Detective Fuller said, as he and Agent Young walked inside the bedroom. He could see the tears running down the agent's face, as she stood staring down at the body. "Is this the partner you spoke of downstairs, Agent Martin?"

"Do the two of you know who's behind this?" another detective asked, as he walked into the bedroom.

"Who the hell are you?" Agent Young asked, looking the new guy over.

Showing his detective badge and introducing himself as Detective Sergeant Aaron Banks, he repeated his question, "Do the two of you know who's behind this, agents?"

"Agent Martin!" Detective Fuller said, "Don't you think it's about time you and Agent Young here begin sharing with me and my partner exactly what's going on here with this murder we've got!"

"You may want to contact Captain Angela Perez, detective," Agent Young told him.

Agent Martin then spoke up. "Or you can help us out, detective. I have an idea how we can get to the bottom of this."

* * *

"Here!" Dante said as he walked into the den, tossing Alinna a black leather wallet and sat down next to Harmony, while she sat watching TV with her legs folded under her.

"What the hell is this?" Alinna asked, as she opened the wallet.

"It belongs to your boyfriend!" Dante told her, watching as Alinna sat starring at the D.E.A. I.D.

"What is this bullshit, Dante?" Alinna asked, holding up the I.D. as she stared angrily at him. "Where the hell you get this shit from?"

"Read the name!" Dante ordered her, just as one of the guards walked over to him and whispered in his ear. Dante nodded his head in understanding and then turned to Vanessa and Dre and said, "Nessa! Dre! Everything ready at y'all new spot. I got y'all right on the other side from this penthouse right here. Harmony and Tony T right under y'all."

"Dante, this is bullshit!" Alinna yelled, as she jumped from the sofa, throwing the wallet at him. Dante simply stared back at her.

Bending down and picking up the wallet, Vanessa opened it and saw the D.E.A. identification for Alex Whitehead. She looked over at Dante and exclaimed, "You was right, Dante! Alex was undercover."

"What the hell?" Alinna said, looking over to her friend. "You know about this shit, too, Vanessa?"

Nodding her head yes, Vanessa went explained about Ben Whitehead the ex-captain and about his son who was Alex Whitehead with D.E.A.

"This is bullshit!" Alinna said, as she stormed from the den cursing and talking shit about Dante and Vanessa and how they were trying to set Alex up because they didn't like him.

"I got her," Vanessa said, as she went after Alinna, catching up with her inside the master bedroom that Dante gave to her and their son, D.J.

"Vanessa, I really don't wanna hear the shit you gotta say," Alinna told her best friend, as she walked back and forth in the middle of the bedroom floor.

Closing the bedroom door, Vanessa turned around and sat on the huge bed.

"Why the fuck can't he just leave me the fuck alone, Vanessa?" Alinna asked, after a few passing minutes. She continued to walk back and forth in front of the bed. "It's been over between me and Dante for months now. Shit! It's been longer than that and his ass still won't leave me the hell alone."

"Do you even really want him to, Alinna?"

"What?" Alinna said, stopping where she was and turning to face Vanessa. "What the hell kind of question is that shit? If you remember, I'm the one who ended things."

"Yeah, that's true, but you're also the one I've seen sleeping with some of his old clothes on or holding D.J. and calling him lil Dante."

"That's bullshit, Vanessa!"

"Is it?" Vanessa asked. "I've seen how you was staring at Dante when he got back. You can talk that shit all you want to and act like you hate that man, but one thing remains the same about you when it comes to Dante. That man will do anything for you because he is still in love with you. Why the hell you think he's back here now? I called him and told him what you told me about that nigga, Fish Man, and here his ass go rushing back here to make sure your ass is okay."

"He came because of all of us? Dante could care less about me. Didn't you just tell me he was with someone else?"

"Truthfully, Alinna. Dante was coming back even before all this shit jumped off with Fish Man and the Haitians. He told me he was coming back because we was throwing you a birthday party this Saturday, and he wanted to be there with you even though you was so caught up in Alex's ass."

Alinna got quiet for a few moments and stared at her best friend. She was unsure of exactly what she was supposed to say. Alinna walked to the sliding glass door in her room and stood staring out over Miami Beach, before she finally spoke: "What's this girl's name who Dante is seeing? And don't tell me you don't know because I see now that he tells you everything."

"Her name's Natalie and she's the daughter of the Dominican drug lord that Dante works for."

"You think he's serious about her?"

"Honestly, Alinna," Vanessa said in a tone that made her turn around and face her, "I think Dante cares for her as much as he does you."

"So, he's in love with her?"

"Maybe! But she's different from you and there's a difference in him because of her. The problem is that he still loves you, Alinna. He may not admit it, but Dante is still in love with you!"

"So, what am I supposed to do?" Alinna asked, as she walked over and sat down next to Vanessa. "I think I've pushed Dante completely away."

"Maybe!" Vanessa replied before adding, "You can change that, Alinna. You know what you gotta do."

18

Dante stood out on the balcony leaning against the rail. He was listening to the line ring as he waited for Natalie to answer, returning a call from earlier. Dante looked back over his shoulder as the sliding door opened and Alinna stepped out onto the balcony with him.

"Dante, we need to talk!" Alinna told him, as she closed the glass sliding door.

Hearing Natalie's voicemail start, he hung up the phone as Alinna stepped up beside him. "What is it now, Alinna?" he asked.

Sighing deeply and softly, she looked out over the city lights. After a moment, she said, "Dante, look! I'm sorry, okay?"

Looking over at Alinna with a surprised expression on his face, Dante laughed lightly as he looked back out over Miami Beach. He began, "Is this where you tell me you wish you wouldn't have met me? Well, you can save it, Alinna! It's clear you hate me, alright!"

"I don't hate you, Dante!" she said, turning to face him. "I know I've been acting really crazy towards you and there's really no way to explain that other than I was hurt and jealous. The truth of it all is that I still love you, Dante!"

She stared at Dante waiting for a response. "Dante, did you hear what I just said?"

"I heard you!"

"So, why didn't you say nothing?"

"What the hell you want me to say, Alinna?" Dante asked angrily, turning to face her. "All this muthafucking time and now you come up with this shit!"

"Do you love me still, Dante?" she asked, ignoring his anger.

Laughing even though nothing was funny, Dante turned away from her and said, "Go away, Alinna! I'm not playing your games anymore!"

Grabbing Dante's arm while snapping him around to face her, she asked, "Dante, tell me the truth! Do you still love me?"

"Yeah, alright!" he answered, snatching away from Alinna saying, "What the fuck do it matter now? I'm already with . . . !"

"Natalie!" Alinna said, cutting him off and seeing the surprised looked on his face for a split second. She continued, "I know about her and I don't care, Dante! I want my family back! Can I have it back?"

Staring at Alinna, Dante opened his mouth to speak when his cell phone went off.

Looking down at the screen, he recognized Dominic's private line. Dante looked at Alinna and said, "I gotta answer this. It's Dominic calling."

"Go ahead!" Alinna told him, as she stepped into Dante and wrapped her arms around him laying her head in his chest.

Caught off guard by Alinna's actions, he decided to allow it for the moment. "Yeah! What's up, Dominic?"

"Dante, how's everything going in Miami so far?" Dominic asked, as soon as he heard Dante's voice.

"So far, so good!" he answered. "Everything good with you and the family? How's Natalie? I missed her phone call and when I tried to call back a few minutes ago, she didn't answer. How is she?"

"Well, Dante! Natalie is actually the reason I'm calling you now. She's here with Carmen and me inside my office. Before I put her on the line I'd like you to tell me something first. What are you feelings towards my daughter, Dante?"

"I love her!" Dante replied, shifting his eyes down to Alinna, as she looked up at him. He focused back on the phone call and continued, "Dominic, what's going on? Where's Natalie?"

"One last question, Dante!" Dominic said, ignoring Dante's question.

"I'm listening!"

"Do you have any plans to my daughter, Dante?"

Quiet for a moment, Dante thought of Alinna and what they were just talking about. He then signed and said, "Truthfully, Dominic, Natalie and I haven't spoken about it but I've thought about it a few times before."

"Well, I'll tell you this, Dante. I love you like you were my own son and I have a lot of respect for you as well. But now that Natalie is pregnant, I expect that you will agree that marriage is the right next step?"

"What?" Dante asked, shocked at what he just heard. "Did you just say that Natalie's pregnant?"

"I did!" Dominic answered. "Here is my daughter, Dante."

Hearing the phone being exchanged, Dante heard Natalie's tear-filled voice: "Dante!"

"Yeah, baby! I'm here!"

"Baby, I'm so sorry. I don't know how this happened."

"Natalie, relax! Relax and calm down!" he told her as calmly as he could. "When did you find out you was pregnant?"

"Earlier today when I noticed I was late on my period. I went and got a test."

"How are you feeling though?"

"I'm fine, Dante!" she answered, "Baby, are you mad at me?"

"Mad...for what? No, I'm not mad, Natalie!"

"When are you coming home?"

"Look! Let me get business here worked out and right after that I'll be home, alright?"

"Alright! I love you!"

"I love you, too, Natalie! Let me talk to Dominic."

"Alright, hold on!" Natalie told Dante.

A few moments later Dominic's voice came over the line. "Yes, Dante?"

"Dominic, alright! I'll be back as soon as I get things worked out here but I need a favor from you."

"Anything for my son-in-law. What is it?"

"I want a business connection with my ba...family here in Miami," Dante told him. "I want you and my family to begin a business relationship."

Quiet a moment, Dominic finally said, "Okay, Dante! I will agree to a business deal of a 45-55 split of whatever your family makes. I will not charge them for my product but they will be expected to pick up here. I will not have my people do all the work. And understand, I do this only because of you."

"Thanks, Dominic!" Dante told the drug lord before realizing had already hung up the phone.

Lowering the phone from his ear, he looked at Alinna. He opened his mouth to speak but she beat him to it. "So I guess D.J. and Mya have either a brother or a sister on the way, huh?"

"Yeah! Pretty much!" Dante answered. He then asked, "You okay?"

"Not really!" Alinna answered, as tears broke loose, running down her face.

Shaking his head as he pulled Alinna against him, Dante wrapped his arms around her while feeling Alinna wrap hers around him. He kissed the top of her head and said, "I'm sorry, Alinna. This shit is crazy right now. I'm really sorry, baby!"

* * *

Unable to sleep, Agent Monica Martin piled through the notes that Agent Alex Whitehead had gathered on Alinna Rodriguez and Dante Blackwell. She sat thinking, trying to figure out what she was going to do. She put off making the phone call to her Agent-in-Command.

Snatching up her Kool cigarettes from the dining room table, she noticed her phone going off. She looked at the screen to see that it was Detective Sergeant Aaron Banks calling her.

"Yes, sergeant!" Agent Martin answered the phone.

"Agent Martin! Myself and my partner thought about your offer and if you can . . ."

"Don't worry, sergeant!" Agent Martin interrupted. "If you're worried about my side of the deal, don't be! I will fully come through on my part. Now, do you accept my offer?"

Quiet for a moment, Detective Banks sighed deeply through the phone before answering, "Alright, Agent Martin. We'll accept the deal!"

19

Dante woke up to the sound of his ringing cell phone. He grabbed at it blindly on the nightstand next to him and answered, "Yeah?"

"Dante! It's Angela!"

"What's up, Angela?" Dante asked, sitting up in bed, instantly remembering where he was. He looked over to his right to see his son and Alinna lying next to him.

"Dante, listen! I don't have much time."

"What's up?"

"Where are you?"

"I'm at home. What's up, Angela?"

"Look! There's been a meeting set up and the chief just called me in. It's something to do with the D.E.A. I'm not sure exactly what's going on, but I'll let you know if it's about you and Alinna once the meeting is over."

"Just to put you up on a little information so you won't go into the meeting blind," Dante told her, "It's probably about homeboy I had you look up for me. He got handled yesterday.

"You mean Alinna's boyfriend?"

"Yeah!" Dante answered. "We'll talk about it later after you get outta the meeting. Where's Mya?"

"Jennifer is on her way to watch her while I'm out."

"Let her know I'ma be by to pick up Mya in a little while."

"Alright! I'll talk to you later, Dante!"

Hearing Angela hang up the phone, Dante tossed his cell back onto the night table. Then Alinna asked, "What does Angela want?"

Looking over to Alinna, he explained to her about Angela's meeting.

Turning to her son after listening to Dante, Alinna bent down and kissed D.J.'s cheek, just as her own cell started to go off.

She picked it up and saw that Vanessa was on the other line. Alinna quickly answered to keep from waking her son. "What now, Nessa?"

"Damn! That how you answer the phone?"

"It is when you calling about to wake up my son! What you want?"

"You seen the news yet?'

"No! Why?"

"You may wanna look at it."

Reaching for the remote, Alinna turned on the wall unit flat screen and turned to a news station. She saw a picture of Alex on the screen. She listened as the reporter discussed the murder of D.E.A. Agent Alex Whitehead, son of murdered Police Captain Bob Whitehead. Alinna continued listening as the reporter said that Alex Whitehead was found with a broken neck with the letters D.E.A. carved into his forehead and the word undercover carved in his chest.

"Alinna, you there?"

Alinna answered her girl, saying she'd call her back and hung up. She looked over at Dante texting on his phone. She asked, "Dante, you did this without telling me. Why?"

Lifting his eyes and looking over to Alinna, Dante met her staring eyes and said, "Would you have listened if I told you that your boyfriend was undercover?"

"So, what now?" Alinna asked, ignoring the question he just asked.

Catching the way she ignored him, Dante let it slide and asked, "You remember the phone call I had last night with Dominic?"

"How couldn't I, Dante?" Alinna replied, rolling her eyes.

"So you heard what I got planned with the family and Dominic."

"I heard what you was telling him. Did he agree, though?"

Breaking down the conversation to Alinna while telling her of Dominic's demands, Dante added, "I've also got two other connects I'ma introduce to you. I don't want you to just depend on Dominic. I'm not sure what he'll do if something happens to me."

"What do you mean 'if something happens to you, Dante?"

Shaking his head, Dante said, "Listen! These two guys are from out of state but they both owe me their life and I want payback."

"Who are they?" Alinna asked, glancing down at D.J., who made a soft sound but rolled over onto his side still asleep.

"One's name is Larry Sutter. He's into heroin and cocaine. The other guy's name is Lorenzo Goldmen. He's also into heroin but he got his hands in cocaine, pills, and a few other things. They both know James so if anything happened to me, James can handle the connection."

"Dante, why do you keep saying if something happens to you? What aren't you telling me?" Alinna wanted to know. She followed him with her eyes as he left the bed and headed into the bathroom.

Alinna heard the shower go on a few minutes later. She got up to join him in the bathroom when her cell phone rang again.

Seeing that it was Amber calling, Alinna took another look at the bathroom before answering. "Yeah, Amber!"

"Alinna, where Dante at?"

"He in the shower, Amber! Why?"

"Tell him that Wesley wanna talk to him about something. He went to handle something, but he'll be back."

"Yeah, alright! I'll talk to you later! I need to handle something, too," Alinna said, hanging up the phone, as she opened the bathroom door.

* * *

As he stood under the showerhead, letting the water beat down on his neck, back, and shoulders, Dante leaned back from under the water when he heard the door open. He looked back to see Alinna completely naked as she stepped into the shower with him.

"We need to talk!" Alinna told him, walking up to Dante as he turned to face her.

"You couldn't have waited until I got out?" he asked as Alinna wrapped her arms up around his neck.

"I want to make love now!" she told him before demanding," Pick me up, Dante!"

Doing as he was asked, Dante lifted Alinna by her ass as she wrapped her legs around his waist and reached down to grab his semi-hard manhood.

"This still belongs to me, right?" she asked, slowly stroking his dick. "I'm not asking you, Dante. I'm telling you that our family is

173

getting back together. I know you have feelings, maybe even love, for this Natalie girl. And because I love you and lost you once, I'll allow you to continue to see her because she's pregnant. But I come first, Dante!"

Sighing, Dante admitted the truth about Dominic's demands. "Alinna! Dominic expects me to marry Natalie now that's she's pregnant. He's actually demanding it!"

"What are you going to . . . ?" Alinna broke off, unable to finish the thought as she closed her eyes and began to moan as Dante's manhood entered her.

Gripping Alinna's hips as she began moving up and down on his dick, Dante backed her up against the shower wall, allowing him to push deeper inside of her.

Alinna lost count after her first orgasm. She came harder each time Dante brought her to climax.

Listening to Alinna scream his name over and over as she dug her fingernails into his upper back, Dante felt himself close to climaxing when Alinna asked, "Dante, will you marry me? Baby, I love you!"

"Shit!" Dante said, exploding deep inside her, pushing and holding himself deep inside of her while Alinna's pussy muscles milked his dick.

"I love you, Dante!" Alinna kept moaning over and over, as she held onto him around his neck.

Once the two of them calmed down and Dante lowered her to her feet, Alinna spoke first, saying, "Dante, I was serious about what I asked you. I want you to marry me."

"What about Natalie?"

"Do you love her, Dante?"

"I can't lie to you, Alinna. Yeah, I love her."

Sighing, Alinna responded, "Alright! Let's move her down here. I can't believe this is coming out of my mouth, but the three of us and D.J. can find a house together."

Staring at Alinna for a moment, Dante asked, "You're serious, aren't you?"

"Dante! I lost you once. I'm not about to let it happen again. If I got to deal with you having another baby momma, then she needs to live with us because I want you here and not outta the state."

Shaking his head and laughing lightly, Dante said, "I gotta talk to Natalie and see what she thinks. But I'm with the plan."

"You better be! Because my family is getting back together and that's not up for discussion!" she told Dante as she turned around and kissed his lips. "Now, let's finish showering! We have things to do today."

* * *

Once Dante and Alinna finished showering, they got dressed. Dante left with James to go pick up Mya. Alinna made some business calls to customers and workers who she knew she could trust.

By the time Alinna finally got out of the bedroom, she barely made it to the front of the penthouse when she heard the doorbell.

Unlocking the door, Alinna opened it and saw Vanessa and Dre standing at the door. She said, "What's up, y'all?"

"Where my brother at?" Vanessa asked as she and Dre entered the penthouse.

Shooting Vanessa, a look back over her shoulder, Alinna rolled her eyes, but said, "He and James sent to pick up Mya. They'll be back soon!"

"Wait a minute!" Vanessa said, smiling as she stopped and stared at Alinna. "What's up with you, girl?"

"What are you talking about" Alinna asked, looking back at Vanessa and seeing the look on her friend's face.

Slowly smiling as she continued staring at Alinna, Vanessa announced, "You slept with Dante!"

Sucking her teeth, Alinna turned away from Vanessa and started to walk away when she grabbed her arm.

"You did, didn't you?" Vanessa asked, as she stepped in front of her. Seeing Alinna trying to hide a smile, Vanessa dragged her behind her to the back bedroom as she called over her shoulder, "You and I gotta talk, and I wanna know everything!"

20

Dante busily spent the day taking care of as much business as he could. He called the new connects he was introducing to Alinna and the family and spoke with Natalie about her moving to Miami to live with him. He explained the possible living arrangements and was shocked when Natalie agreed to Dante's proposal. After that, Dante finally made it to Angela's house and picked up his daughter.

"Daddy, where's my brother?" Mya asked from the back seat of Dante's Benz.

"We're going to where D.J. is now, baby girl!" Dante answered, smiling back at his daughter. "You hungry?"

"Yes!" She replied. "Can I have McDonald's, daddy?"

Still smiling, Dante looked over to James and said, "Find a McDonald's, J!"

After a successful trip to McDonald's with Happy Meals for Mya and D.J., James finally made it back to the tower. He parked inside the garage and took the elevator up to the penthouse.

Nodding to security as he followed Mya off the elevator, Dante laid his hand on his daughter's back as she watched the guards. Then he led her to the penthouse door.

Unlocking and opening the front door to the penthouse, Dante allowed Mya to enter first. He then followed inside, with James walking in behind.

"Alinna!" Dante yelled, as he followed Mya to the kitchen. He watched the way his daughter looked around the place.

"Yeah, baby!" Alinna answered, breaking out in a smile at seeing Dante and the beautiful little girl.

"Mya!" Dante called to his daughter. "I want you to meet Alinna. She's D.J.'s mother."

Looking from Dante to Alinna and then back to her father, Mya slowly looked at Alinna and said, "Is my brother here?"

Smiling back at the little girl, Alinna called her son. Upon hearing him in the den, Alinna called, "D.J., come to the kitchen, sweetheart. Your sister is here!"

Hearing D.J.'s bare feet running across the tile floor, Dante smiled when his son saw his sister. Breaking out in a smile as well, D.J. walked up to Mya and hugged her.

Alinna smiled as she watched the two children playing and talking to each other. Mya took her brother's hand, looked up at Dante, and asked for their food. Alinna smiled a little harder as both children left the kitchen together, talking with the type of affection she found herself close to crying over.

"You alright?" Dante asked, as he walked up behind Alinna and wrapped his arms around her from behind.

Leaning back into Dante, Alinna tilted her head back and kissed him a moment. The she broke the kiss by saying, "Everybody's in the den. I made sure they made contact with the workers and buyers. I also explained what you told me about the new contact but I left out anything about Dominic in case you didn't want to mention it yet."

"That's my girl!" Dante replied. "I also called Natalie and she agreed to come to Miami. And I talked to both Sutter and Goldmen, the new connects. They'll be here next week to meet with us. But you're in control and it's you they will be looking to talk to. Be ready though, because they're sending a shipment down ahead of them to thank me."

"Let me guess!" Alinna said, smiling up at Dante. "You made a deal with them instead of killing them, right?"

"Something like that!" Dante answered with a smile.

"Ummm...excuse me!" Vanessa interrupted, smiling at catching both of them. "I'm happy the two of you are back together but if you don't mind, we have things to discuss. For example, this birthday party that's tomorrow night. Thank you!"

Shaking his head and smiling as Alinna stood lightly laughing, Dante watched Vanessa leave the kitchen and head in the direction of the den.

* * *

Joining the others in the den, Dante and Alinna sat together on the loveseat and began discussing issues that concerned their business. Dante re-explained what Alinna had told the family about the new connect. He then went deeper and made sure that everyone understood that James was Alinna's personal bodyguard. If anything happened to him or if he needed to leave to go back to Phoenix for a while, James would make sure everything went smoothly with the new connects.

Alinna began discussing the continuing issue with Fish Man and the Haitians. She moved on after a while to the issue concerning the D.E.A. Alinna mentioned Alex Whitehead's supposed sister, Monica when Dante chipped in that he was waiting for Angela to call and would ask about Monica then.

Once all the issues were out of the way, Vanessa mentioned Alinna's birthday party at Club Empire. She explained that there were still a few other things left to handle before the party.

Hearing his cell phone go off inside his pocket, Dante dug out the phone and saw that Angela was finally getting back to him.

"I'ma be right back," Dante told Alinna, as he stood up from his seat and walked out of the den on his phone. "Yeah, Angela. What's up?"

"Hey Dante! Where are you?"

"At home! Why? What's up?"

"Okay, look! I just left the meeting at the station with the chief and the D.E.A. The D.E.A. has agreed to back off for the moment because of Whitehead's death while his partner doesn't want to take the case for some reason. She says she can't deal with the case right now."

"Wait! That's something I wanna ask you now that you mention it. What's Whitehead's partner's name?"

"Monica Martin. But they also had a third agent by the name of Paul Young. Why you ask?"

"Alinna mentioned Whitehead's sister's name was Monica. But I see now that she was undercover, too."

"Well, I'm glad I had a talk with Martin after the meeting then because although I don't gamble, I'm willing to bet that Alinna didn't know that Monica Martin was more than Whitehead's partner. She was his wife, and they had two daughters and a son together. They were only married five years before Whitehead died, so if I had to guess, Dante . . ."

". . . This just became personal!" Dante finished for Angela.

"Pretty much!" she answered. "So, what's the plan now?"

Quiet a moment in thought, Dante finally said, "Find out everything you can on Monica Martin and let me know. I'll deal with her myself."

"Alright, sweetheart! I'll get started on that tonight, but it'll probably take a while."

"Just let me know when you get something."

"I will!" she answered. "You keeping Mya tonight or are you bringing her home?"

"She staying with me! I'll bring her home tomorrow afternoon."

Hanging up with Angela and heading back into the den as everyone was getting ready to leave, Dante got in his goodbyes and received kisses from Amber, Harmony, and Vanessa.

After the others left, Dante told Alinna he would talk to her in the bedroom. First, though, he pulled James outside onto the balcony to talk with him.

"What's up, bro?" James asked, as Dante closed the sliding glass door.

Turning to face James, Dante stepped up to the rail beside him and said, "Bruh, listen! You know I trust you with my life, which means I trust you with Alinna and my kids lives as well. Shit about to get crazy from all sides and I'm not sure how it's gonna end up with me. But I need your word that no matter what, you'll protect my family."

"Bro, come on! That's not even a question. I got you, but tell me what's going on so I can be on point, too!" James told him, staring straight at Dante.

Dante then proceeded to tell James about Monica Martin and Paul Young with the D.E.A., and everything Angela told him. He also broke down his feelings concerning the end of how things would play out for him.

"Relax, bro! It may not play out how you think it will!" James told him, dropping his arm around Dante's shoulder.

* * *

"Baby, you alright?" Alinna asked Dante, as soon as he walked into the bedroom

"Yeah!" Dante answered, as he kicked off his shoes and sat down on the bed. "I'm just trying to get my mind right, Alinna."

"What's bothering you?"

After telling Alinna about Monica Martin and Paul Young, Dante added, "I think she's making this shit personal since Whitehead's dead now."

"So, what are we going to do?"

"I got Angela checking out a few things for me. We'll find out what the next play is then."

"Daddy!" D.J. and Mya cried out, as they both ran into the bedroom laughing with the maid right behind them.

"It's okay, Rose!" Alinna told the older woman, as she smiled at the kids jumping around with Dante, who was laughing as he got into kid mode with them.

Smiling and watching Dante with the kids, Alinna felt a tear stream down the side of her cheek.

Hating what she had allowed to happen between her and Dante, Alinna swore to herself that nothing would ever get her to turn her back on the man she loved.

* * *

Gathering the kids and James, Alinna and Dante took them to the mall, spoiling them with much more than they needed. Alinna also got a new outfit to wear to her birthday party.

Alinna went to try on an outfit but when she came out of the changing room, Dante and the kids were gone. Only James was waiting for her a few feet away. She walked over to him and asked, "James, where'd Dante and the kids go?"

"He just said he would be back!"

"That's all he said?"

"Yep."

Staring at the smirk on James face, Alinna rolled her eyes. Then she looked over her shoulder before heading back to the changing room and telling James, "You're turning out to be just like your boy, Dante!"

"Thanks!" James loudly replied, which caused Alinna to lightly laugh and glance back at him.

After changing back into her own clothes, Alinna paid for all the items she was going to buy and left the store with James.

"Call Dante and find out where he is, James!" Alinna told him, as she stepped in front of a display window two doors down from the store she and James had just left.

Alinna walked into a jewelry store and walked up to the counter. She asked to see the white gold and diamond studded, Cuban link chain and cross. It had a tilting crown that sat at the tip of the cross with the word boss written out in diamonds across the front of the crown.

Alinna didn't flinch at the price and bought the chain without a second thought. Then she followed alongside James a few minutes later after her purchase was wrapped and boxed up for her.

"Where did Dante say he . . . ?

"Damn, baby! What's up?"

Looking down at the hand that was holding her arm and stopping her from walking, Alinna looked up at the creep and said, "First, I ain't your baby! Second, you better get ya nasty-ass hands off me before you get fucked up in this mall in front of everybody."

"What?" the guy said surprised. "Bitch, who the fuck . . .?

Alinna watched as James swiftly stepped in, slamming two quick blows to the guy's stomach and one to the guy's temple, sending him to the ground. Alinna continued watching as James picked back up all her bags and calmly said, "You ready to go?"

Smiling slowly as she continued walking again, Alinna said to James, "That was pretty impressive! You kind of fight a little like Dante."

"Not that much!" James replied. "I fought against Dante in a contest. The boy got skills for real."

"He won?" Alinna asked, just as she heard D.J.'s voice calling out to her.

Looking back over her shoulder at her son running over toward her, Alinna broke out in a smile as she set down her bags. She bent down to catch D.J. just as he threw himself into her arms. "Hey you!"

"Momma, daddy bought me and Mya matching chains," D.J. told his mother, holding up the gold and platinum chain and heart locket.

"It's beautiful, sweetheart!" Alinna told her son, as she opened the locket and find a picture of Mya and D.J. together smiling as they hugged each other.

"Daddy bought me one, too!" Mya said, causing Alinna to look up just as Mya and Dante walked up.

Looking at the picture inside of Mya's locket, Alinna found a picture of D.J. Alinna looked up to Dante confusedly who simply said, "She just wanted a picture of her brother alone."

"Well, it's still beautiful!" Alinna said, smiling as she kissed Mya on the cheek.

"I just saw some dude laid out back there with a crowd around him. You two had something to do with that back there?" Dante asked, looking from Alinna over to a smirking James.

"I'm hungry," Alinna announced as she picked up her bags. "Can we get something to eat please, Mr. Blackwell?"

Shaking his head and still smiling, James spoke up once Dante looked back at him: "I'm not buying, bro! She your woman and she asked you!"

21

Alinna woke up to find Dante and the kids already gone. She smelled food, which made her smile. She climbed out of bed wearing one of Dante's t-shirts and headed to the front of the penthouse.

"Good morning, Alinna!" Rose said, smiling when she saw the younger woman enter the kitchen.

"Hey Rose!" Alinna replied, looking around. "Where's Dante and the kids?"

"Dante took both D.J. and Mya out for breakfast and asked me to cook you breakfast this morning. He also asked that I tell you to relax inside the hot tub and expect him home later. Oh, and I almost forgot. This is for you!"

Seeing the long, wide black velvet box that Rose picked up from the counter top, Alinna broke out in a smile as she walked over and grabbed the present from Rose.

"Dante left this for you!" Rose told her smiling. "He says this is one of the three birthday gifts he has for you."

Alinna smiled as she opened the box. Her mouth dropped wide open at seeing the 14k strawberry gold Gucci chain. It had vanilla diamonds wrapped around a larger chocolate diamond and chocolate diamond studs. "This man is too much, Rose!"

"I think he's perfect for you, if you ask me!" the maid told Alinna, smiling at her boss and friend.

Alinna found herself in the bedroom moments later, sitting on the bed trying to get a hold of Dante.

"Yeah!" Dante answered, after the second ring.

"Hey, baby! Where are you?"

"With the kids! You got your present?"

"Yes!" she answered, smiling harder. "Thank you. I love it, Dante."

"Happy birthday!" he told her. "Now I want you to go ahead and hop inside the hot tub and relax. Rose will take care of everything until I get there."

"When are you getting here?"

"Soon!" Dante answered.

Smiling while shaking her head as she laid the cell phone on the bed, Alinna looked up just as Rose entered the bedroom with a serving tray and food.

Alinna thanked Rose as she sat the tray on the bed. Shortly after Rose left the bedroom, Alinna heard the hot tub jets start bubbling.

* * *

Accidentally falling back asleep, Alinna woke up to feeling someone kissing her lips. She opened her eyes to see Dante smiling at the simple sight of her. She said, "Hey, baby! What time is it?"

"It's 9:30 and time for you to get up so we can start getting ready!" Dante told her, sitting down as Alinna sat up and wrapped her arms around his neck, kissing him on the cheek.

"Where's D.J. and Mya?" Alinna asked, as she sat up holding onto Dante.

"I sent them with Rose over to Angela's house for the night," he answered. "Come on! Let's get up because I'm pretty sure Vanessa gonna call back in a few minutes."

"How many times has she called?"

"I lost count!"

Standing back up from the bed, Dante bent over and kissed Alinna's lips again and he headed towards the bathroom.

Alinna watched Dante until he walked into the bathroom. She smiled as she climbed out of bed to begin getting ready.

* * *

After 20 minutes, Alinna was fully dressed in a cream-colored Dolce and Gabbana full-body skirt with matching stiletto heels.

She was sliding on her floor length, black fur coat that Dante had bought her.

"You look gorgeous!" Dante told her, walking into the bedroom and looking over Alinna hungrily.

Alinna stared back at Dante just as hard, as he walked out wearing a cream Stacy Adams three-piece suit with a sky blue dress shirt and pin stripe white and sky-blue neck time. Alinna walked over to him, reached up, and fixed the collar of the white floor length overcoat he was wearing. "You are the most handsome man I've ever known, Dante Blackwell."

Winking at her, Dante held out his hand and asked, "You ready?"

Grabbing her handbag and her phone, Alinna walked over and took Dante's hand. "I'm ready, baby!"

Leaving the penthouse, Alinna and Dante rode the elevator down to the first floor lobby, where two security guards waited to escort them out of the building following Dante's head nod of approval.

"Oh, my God!" Alinna said in shock when she saw the pearl-white and cream-colored Rolls Royce Phantom parked in front of the building.

"Happy birthday!" Dante said, smiling down at her.

"What? Dante, is this for me?" Alinna asked in disbelief, staring from the Phantom to Dante.

"It's your second gift!" he told her, still smiling. "You like it?"

Throwing her arms up around Dante's neck, Alinna hugged him tight before releasing him and turning to the car. She noticed James standing at the back door dressed in a stylish black and white suit smiling back at her.

"Come on!" Dante said, smiling as he walked Alinna over to the Phantom. James opened the back door for them.

"Happy birthday!" James said, as Alinna climbed into the back of the car.

Once Alinna sat down on the cream-colored leather seats, she couldn't help smiling as she took in the details of the interior.

* * *

Five minutes after receiving Dante's text message, letting her know they were on their way to the nightclub with Alinna, Vanessa walked through the packed club to find Amber and Harmony. They chatted with friends, business associates, and members of the crew and their families.

Making their way to the balcony that overlooked the club, which could hold around twenty people, Vanessa entered first. She smiled when she saw Dre standing at the rail with a bottle of Hennessy gripped in his hand as he stared down at the crowd.

Breaking off from her girls and making her way over to Dre, Vanessa stepped beside her man, wrapped her arms around his waist, and said, "What's up, you?"

Dre leaned towards Vanessa, kissed her, and said, "You did your thing with setting this party up tonight. It's packed as hell in here."

"Amber and Harmony helped me out with most of . . . !"

Vanessa broke off what she was saying when she noticed the crowd and security rushing towards the front doors. She swung her head around when she heard her name and saw Harmony and Amber with two security guards.

"What the hell happened now?" Dre asked, as he and Vanessa walked over.

"Vanessa, we got a problem!" Harmony started. "Both Wesley and Tony T already went down but you know how those two are."

"What's happening?" Vanessa asked.

"It's Fish Man and some Haitians!" Amber answered, just as Dre took off towards the stairs, dropping the Hennessy bottle he was holding to the ground.

"Come on!" Vanessa yelled, as she took off behind Dre.

Once downstairs, Dre and Vanessa pushed their way through the crowd. They saw their team of security and crewmembers standing around both Tony T and Wesley as they stood facing down Fish Man, a heavy-set Haitian man and his posse of Haitians surrounding him.

"Mutherfucka, you gotta be ready to die!" Dre said as he pushed to the front next to Tony T, his banger already in his hand.

"Well, here we go!" Fish Man said, ignoring Dre, Wesley, and Tony T. He smiled at Vanessa, Amber, and Harmony. "I was wondering when you bitches would show up!"

Grabbing Dre before he could rush at Fish Man, Vanessa said, "What the fuck do you want, nigga?"

"Da blood clot fool want to die!" Wesley said, gripping his burner and anxious to get things turned up.

"Where's Alinna?" Fish Man said, still ignoring the guys.

"She not here!" Vanessa answered. "How the fuck you even know we would be here?"

"Everybody know about the bitch's birthday party!" Fish Man responded. "By the way, let me introduce you to your new boss. Meet Zoe Papi!"

"You gotta be crazy!" Tony T said, laughing in Fish Man and Zoe's faces.

"Vanessa!" Amber called, as she got her attention and nodded towards the parking lot.

Vanessa turned and saw the new Phantom pulling into the club.

Vanessa turned back toward Fish Man and said, "You was looking for Alinna! Well, here she come now!"

Turning his attention to the Rolls Royce Phantom that was slowly pulling up, Fish Man smiled. He was very impressed with the bitch's style.

Fish Man watched as the car stopped and a white man climbed out from behind the driver's seat. He walked around and opened the door, as Alinna Rodriguez climbed out of the Phantom. He then said, "The bitch herself finally decided to show the fuck up. What took you so damn long?"

"Why don't you ask him?" Alinna answered, as she stepped to the side from in front of the car door.

"What the fuck!" Fish Man said, instantly recognizing the guy climbing out of the Phantom and walking over to stand in front of him. "W-what the hell you doing here? I thought you two broke up!"

"That's the problem with thinking. You should first learn how to!" Dante replied. "Here's the deal! You got two choices. One is you can leave Miami now! Leave Florida tonight. Your second choice is you can die right here, right now! Decide now!"

"Mutha . . . !"

Dante snatched his banger from his right shoulder holster in his left hand and swung it over. He landed the barrel of the heater on the point of the heavy-set guy's nose before anyone realized what was happening. As he cut Fish Man off, he shifted his eyes slowly over to the other guy and asked, "Who the fuck are you?"

Hearing someone scream in pain, Dante saw James tuck a chrome banger inside the front of his pants and move back to stand next to Alinna as one of Fish Man's men fell over.

"I'm waiting for an answer!" Dante told the heavy guy looking back at him.

"I'm Zoe Papi!" he replied, staring Dante straight in the eyes.

Slowly smirking, Dante said, "So, you're the Haitian who's with this clown, Fish Man, huh? Well, here's my offer to you. Since Fish Bitch about to either leave for good out of Florida or die, I'm pretty sure you wanna continue business, correct?"

"You offering?" Papi asked in his Haitian accent?

"Alinna!" Dante called.

"Yeah!" Alinna answered from behind him.

"What do you say? You offering Zoe Papi a business deal or what?" Dante asked, maintaining eye contact with the Haitian.

"We can talk business tomorrow! Leave me with your contact info," Alinna told him.

"What do you say, Zoe Papi?" Dante asked. "Do we have a deal or what?"

Slowly nodding his head yes, Papi called out to his men to load up as he explained that they were leaving. Then he looked over at Alinna to let her know he had her number and would be calling the next day.

"Whoa!" Dante said as he grabbed the back of Fish Man's jacket and snapped him back around as he turned to leave. "You still have a decision to make and I'm tired of waiting for an answer. Decide now!"

Fish Man looked from Dante to his own crew as they awaited a decision from their boss. "Alright! I'm outta here! I'll leave Florida tonight!"

"Good decision!" Dante replied, smirking as he smacked Fish Man across the face.

22

After Fish Man and the Haitians left, Dante and Alinna followed the family inside the club up to the V.I.P. section where their friends and crewmembers were waiting.

Dante allowed Alinna to spend some time with her girls, as he kept catching her eyes with his glances. Dante then slid his hand inside his right pants pocket as he felt for the box he had put there.

"What's up, family?" Dre said, as he, Wesley, Tony T, and James walked over to stand next to him by the rail.

"What's good, family?" Dante replied, smiling at his boys while still shifting his eyes back towards Alinna as she looked at him with a smile.

"So, it's real then?" Dre asked, getting Dante's attention. "You and Alinna back at it, huh?"

Nodding his head yes, Dante answered, "Yeah, bruh! We giving it another try!"

"You sure about this?" Dre asked.

Looking to Dre and meeting the look in his eyes, Dante nodded his head and said, "She ya sister, bruh! That's not changing."

Turning his attention over to the others, he saw Vanessa and Harmony carrying a cake. Amber walked behind them pushing a cart with an even larger cake atop it. Dante shook his head and smiled. He walked over with the rest of his boys and started singing "Happy Birthday" to Alinna.

Alinna smiled as she looked around at everyone singing before locking eyes with Dante and mouthing the words "I love you" to him as the song ended.

Making a wish, Alinna blew out the candles on the smaller cake. Then, with the family's help, she blew out the candles on the larger cake.

"Girl, what you wish for?" Harmony asked, smiling as she held onto Tony T.

"I have everything I . . ."

"Naw!" Dante interrupted, walking over to stand beside her. "You can't say you got everything yet since you still missing one thing!"

"What are you...h my God, Dante!" Alinna cried, as she watched Dante get down on one knee and smile at her.

"Yeah, I know this a surprise, huh?" Dante said, still smiling up at Alinna. "I remember you asking me a question a while again. You asked why I love you. Well, to answer that I'd have to say it's because you first loved me and actually showed me how to love you back in return. I never had any woman like you in my life before and I honestly don't wanna live if I can't live life without you in it or a part of it. Will you marry me, Alinna Rodriguez?"

"Yes!" Alinna cried, as tears slid down her face. She threw her arms around Dante's neck, hugging him tightly while still happily crying.

He put the strawberry and chocolate diamond ring on her finger, which caused Alinna to break down crying even harder. Dante received a quick hug before Alinna was pulled away from him.

Getting back to his feet, his boys crowded around him as Alinna went to celebrate with her girls.

"Everybody, freeze! This is the Miami Dade Police Department!"

"What the fuck!" Dre said.

Taking off towards the rail just in time to see a team of police rushing up the stairs, Dante spun around just as the first plain-clothed officer rushed into the V.I.P. section waving his badge.

"Alinna Rodriguez, you're under arrest!" the officer said, as he walked straight over to Alinna and grabbed her.

Never seeing the guy dressed in white fly across the room until it was too late, the plain-clothed officer found himself being thrown into his back up officer.

He snatched both bangers while the family, crew, and security all pulled out their heaters. Dante was a second away from letting his gun's bark when he heard his name yelled.

"Wait!" Agent Martin yelled, as she pushed through the team of officers and held up her D.E.A. I.D. "Dante, tell your people to wait! Let's talk about this."

"Who the fuck are you?" Dante asked, staring at the woman rather than her I.D.

"Monica!" Alinna said, recognizing the woman in front of her and Dante.

Upon hearing her name Dante figured out what was going on and nearly pulled his trigger.

"Dante, wait! Let's make a deal! We'll leave Alinna alone if you agree to come with us."

"Hell no!" Alinna yelled. Snatching the extra gun from James' waist, she swung it up and towards Monica, yelling, "Bitch, you not taking Dante no fucking where!"

"Dante, is this what you want?" Monica asked, ignoring Alinna. "I give you my word. You come with us and I'll make sure Alinna is left alone."

"Dante, don't even . . . !"

"If I agree to this shit and anyone of these muthafuckas touch her, you'll be the first to die! We clear?" Dante asked, cutting Alinna off.

"Dante, what the hell are you doing?" Alinna asked, grabbing his arm.

"Are we clear, Agent Martin?" Dante asked again as he stared straight at Monica.

"We clear!" Monica answered, holding back a smile she felt pulling at her lips.

"Hell no!" Alinna yelled. She went to swing the banger at Monica but Dante stepped between them.

"Dante, what the hell are you doing?"

"Just trust me!" Dante told her before handing both bangers to James and saying, "J, remember what I told you. I trust you with her life so make sure she stay safe!"

"You sure about this, Dante, man?" James asked.

"Just look after my family! I'ma be alright!" Dante told James, before turning to an angered Alinna. "I'm pretty sure I don't have to tell you to hold shit together while I'm gone, right?"

"Dante, don't do this shit!" Alinna begged. She accepted the kiss he gave her before he turned and faced Monica.

"Alright, Agent Martin. Let's get this shit over with!" Dante told her, as two plain-clothed officers stepped up and roughly grabbed his arm.

"Not so bad now are you, asshole?" one officer said, smirking while his partner handcuffed Dante.

Smashing the crown of his head into the officer's nose, Dante heard the bone break as the officer yelled out in pain. Dante smiled as he grabbed his bleeding nose. "I'm a let this shit happen, but you ain't about to be talking shit, muthafucker!"

Watching Dante calmly walk out of the V.I.P. area surrounded by police officer, Alinna saw Monica smiling. "How does it feel, bitch? Now you losing Dante, just like I lost my partner!"

"You mean your husband, right?" Alinna replied, smirking at seeing the surprised look on Monica's face. "Oh, you thought I didn't know you and Alex was married, huh? Tell me, something though. How did my pussy taste? Alex loved eating that shit."

"Bitch!" Monica yelled, swinging at Alinna but failing as James intervened, sending Monica falling into a chair.

She looked up to multiple guns pointed at her while James stood guarded in front of Alinna. She slowly stood up and backed her way towards the stairs. As she left she yelled to Alinna, "I'ma make sure Dante's ass gets life for killing Alex. I promise you that, bitch!"

To be continued

BOOKS BY GOOD2GO AUTHORS

GOOD 2 GO FILMS PRESENTS

**THE HAND I WAS DEALT- FREE WEB SERIES
NOW AVAILABLE ON YOUTUBE!
YOUTUBE.COM/SILKWHITE212**

SEASON TWO NOW AVAILABLE

To order books, please fill out the order form below:

To order films please go to www.good2gofilms.com

Name:_____

Address:_____

City: _____ State: _____ Zip Code: _____

Phone:_____

Email:_____

Method of Payment: Check   VISA   MASTERCARD

Credit Card#:_____

Name as it appears on card: _____

Signature: _____

Item Name	Price	Qty	Amount
48 Hours to Die – Silk White	$14.99		
Business Is Business – Silk White	$14.99		
Business Is Business 2 – Silk White	$14.99		
Business Is Business 3 – Silk White	$14.99		
Childhood Sweethearts – Jacob Spears	$14.99		
Childhood Sweethearts 2 – Jacob Spears	$14.99		
Childhood Sweethearts 3 - Jacob Spears	$14.99		
Flipping Numbers – Ernest Morris	$14.99		
Flipping Numbers 2 – Ernest Morris	$14.99		
He Loves Me, He Loves You Not - Mychea	$14.99		
He Loves Me, He Loves You Not 2 - Mychea	$14.99		
He Loves Me, He Loves You Not 3 - Mychea	$14.99		
He Loves Me, He Loves You Not 4 – Mychea	$14.99		
He Loves Me, He Loves You Not 5 – Mychea	$14.99		
Lost and Turned Out – Ernest Morris	$14.99		
Married To Da Streets – Silk White	$14.99		
M.E.R.C. - Make Every Rep Count Health and Fitness	$14.99		
My Besties – Asia Hill	$14.99		
My Besties 2 – Asia Hill	$14.99		
My Besties 3 – Asia Hill	$14.99		
My Besties 4 – Asia Hill	$14.99		
My Boyfriend's Wife - Mychea	$14.99		
My Boyfriend's Wife 2 – Mychea	$14.99		
Never Be The Same – Silk White	$14.99		
Stranded – Silk White	$14.99		
Slumped – Jason Brent	$14.99		
Tears of a Hustler - Silk White	$14.99		
Tears of a Hustler 2 - Silk White	$14.99		
Tears of a Hustler 3 - Silk White	$14.99		
Tears of a Hustler 4- Silk White	$14.99		
Tears of a Hustler 5 – Silk White	$14.99		
Tears of a Hustler 6 – Silk White	$14.99		
The Panty Ripper - Reality Way	$14.99		

The Panty Ripper 3 – Reality Way	$14.99		
The Teflon Queen – Silk White	$14.99		
The Teflon Queen 2 – Silk White	$14.99		
The Teflon Queen 3 – Silk White	$14.99		
The Teflon Queen 4 – Silk White	$14.99		
The Teflon Queen 5 – Silk White	$14.99		
The Teflon Queen 6 - Silk White	$14.99		
Tied To A Boss - J.L. Rose	$14.99		
Tied To A Boss 2 - J.L. Rose	$14.99		
Time Is Money - Silk White	$14.99		
Young Goonz – Reality Way	$14.99		
Subtotal:			
Tax:			
Shipping (Free) U.S. Media Mail:			
Total:			

Make Checks Payable To:
Good2Go Publishing
7311 W Glass Lane,
Laveen, AZ 85339

35674056712178

CPSIA information can be obtained at www.ICGtesting.com
Printed in the USA
LVOW10s1449071016

507864LV00013B/440/P